A Problem in Greek Ethics
By John Addington Symonds

PREFACE.

THE following treatise on Greek Love was written in the year 1873, when my mind was occupied with my *Studies of Greek Poets*. I printed ten copies of it privately in 1883. It was only when I read the Terminal Essay appended by Sir Richard Burton to his translation of the *Arabian Nights* in 1886, that I became aware of M. H. E. Meier's article on *Pæderastie* (Ersch and Gruber's *Encyclopædie*, Leipzig, Brockhaus, 1837). My treatise, therefore, is a wholly independent production. This makes Meier's agreement (in Section 7 of his article) with the theory I have set forth in Section X, regarding the North Hellenic origin of Greek Love, and its Dorian character, the more remarkable. That two students, working separately upon the same mass of material, should have arrived at similar conclusions upon this point strongly confirms the probability of the hypothesis.

J. A. SYMONDS.

CONTENTS.

--------:o:--------

I. INTRODUCTION: Method of treating the subject.

II. Homer had no knowledge of paiderastia--Achilles--Treatment of Homer by the later Greeks.

III. The Romance of Achilles and Patroclus.

IV. The heroic ideal of masculine love.

V. Vulgar paiderastia--How introduced into Hellas--Crete--Laius--The myth of Ganymede.

VI. Discrimination of two loves, heroic and vulgar. The mixed sort is the paiderastia defined as Greek love in this essay.

VII. The intensity of paiderastia as an emotion, and its quality.

VIII. Myths of paiderastia.

IX. Semi-legendary tales of love--Harmodius and Aristogeiton.

X. Dorian Customs--Sparta and Crete--Conditions of Dorian life--Moral quality of Dorian love--Its final degeneracy--Speculations on the early Dorian *Ethos*--Bœotians' customs--The sacred band--Alexander the Great--Customs of Elis and Megara--*Hybris*--Ionia.

XI. Paiderastia in poetry of the lyric age. Theognis and Kurnus--Solon--Ibycus, the male Sappho--Anacreon and Smerdies--Drinking songs--Pindar and Theoxenos--Pindar's lofty conception of adolescent beauty.

XII. Paiderastia upon the Attic stage--*Myrmidones* of Æschylus--*Achilles' lovers*, and *Niobe* of Sophocles--The *Chrysippus* of Euripides--Stories about Sophocles--Illustrious Greek paiderasts.

XIII. Recapitulation of points--Quotation from the speech of Pausanias on love in Plato's *Symposium*--Observations on this speech. Position of women at Athens--Attic notion of marriage as a duty--The institution of *Paidagogi*--Life of a Greek boy--

Aristophanes' *Clouds*--Lucian's *Amores*--The Palæstra--The *Lysis*--The *Charmides*--Autolycus in Xenophon's *Symposium*--Speech of Critobulus on beauty and love--Importance of gymnasia in relation to paiderastia--Statues of Erôs--Cicero's opinions--Laws concerning the gymnasia--Graffiti on walls--Love-poems and panegyrics--Presents to boys--Shops and *mauvais lieux*--Paiderastic *Hetaireia*--Brothels--Phædon and Agathocles. Street brawls about boys--*Lysias in Simonem*.

XIV. Distinctions drawn by Attic law and custom--*Chrestoi Pornoi*--Presents and money--Atimia of freemen who had sold their bodies--The definition of *Misthosis*--*Eromenos, Hetairekos, Peporneumenos*, distinguished--*Æschines against Timarchus*--General conclusion as to Attic feeling about honourable paiderastia.

XV. Platonic doctrine on Greek love--The asceticism of the *Laws*--Socrates--His position defined by Maximus Tyrius--His science of erotics--The theory of the *Phædrus*: erotic *Mania*--The mysticism of the *Symposium*: love of beauty--Points of contact between Platonic paiderastia and chivalrous love: *Mania* and Joie: Dante's *Vita Nuova*--Platonist and Petrarchist--Gibbon on the "thin device" of the Athenian philosophers--Testimony of Lucian, Plutarch, Cicero.

XVI. Greek liberty and Greek love extinguished at Chæronea--The Idyllists--Lucian's *Amores*--Greek poets never really gross--*Mousa Paidiké*--Philostratus' *Epistolai Erotikai*--Greek Fathers on paiderastia.

XVII. The deep root struck by paiderastia in Greece--Climate--Gymnastics--Syssitia--Military life-Position of Women: inferior culture; absence from places of resort--Greek leisure.

XVIII. Relation of paiderastia to the fine arts--Greek sculpture wholly and healthily human--Ideals of female deities--Paiderastia did not degrade the imagination of the race--Psychological analysis underlying Greek mythology--The psychology of love--Greek mythology fixed before Homer--Opportunities enjoyed by artists for studying women--Anecdotes about artists--The æsthetic temperament of the Greeks, unbiassed by morality and religion, encouraged paiderastia--*Hora*--Physical and moral qualities admired, by a Greek--Greek ethics were esthetic--*Sophrosyne*--Greek religion was æsthetic--No notion of Jehovah--Zeus and Ganymede.

XIX. Homosexuality among Greek women--Never attained to the same dignity as paiderastia.

XX. Greek love did not exist at Rome--Christianity--Chivalry--The *modus vivendi* of the modern world.

A PROBLEM IN GREEK ETHICS.

I.

FOR the student of sexual inversion, ancient Greece offers a wide field for observation and reflection. Its importance has hitherto been underrated by medical and legal writers on the subject, who do not seem to be aware that here alone in history have we the example of a great and highly-developed race not only tolerating homosexual passions, but deeming them of spiritual value, and attempting to utilise them for the benefit of society. Here, also, through the copious stores of literature at our disposal, we can arrive at something definite regarding the various forms assumed by these passions, when allowed free scope for development in the midst of a refined and intellectual civilisation. What the Greeks called paiderastia, or boy-love, was a phenomenon of one of the most brilliant periods of human culture, in one of the most highly organised and nobly active nations. It is the feature by which Greek social life is most sharply distinguished from that of any other people approaching the Hellenes in moral or mental distinction. To trace the history of so remarkable a custom in their several communities, and to ascertain, so far as this is possible, the ethical feeling of the Greeks upon this subject, must be of service to the scientific psychologist. It enables him to approach the subject from another point of view than that usually adopted by modern jurists, psychiatrists, writers on forensic medicine.

II.

The first fact which the student has to notice is that in the Homeric poems a modern reader finds no trace of this passion. It is true that Achilles, the hero of the *Iliad*, is distinguished by his friendship for Patroclus no less emphatically than Odysseus, the hero of the *Odyssey*, by lifelong attachment to Penelope, and Hector by love for Andromache. But in the delineation of the friendship of Achilles and Patroclus there is nothing which indicates the passionate relation of the lover and the beloved, as they were afterwards recognised in Greek society. This is the more remarkable because the love of Achilles for Patroclus added, in a later age of Greek history, an almost religious sanction to the martial form of paiderastia. In like manner the friendship of Idomeneus for Meriones, and that of Achilles, after the death of Patroclus, for Antilochus, were treated by the later Greeks as paiderastic. Yet, inasmuch as Homer gives no warrant for this interpretation of the tales in question, we are justified in concluding that homosexual relations were not prominent in the so-called heroic age of Greece. Had it formed a distinct feature of the society depicted in the Homeric poems, there is no reason to suppose that their authors would have abstained from delineating it. We shall see that Pindar, Æschylus and Sophocles, the poets of an age when paiderastia was prevalent, spoke unreservedly upon the subject.

Impartial study of the *Iliad* leads us to the belief that the Greeks of the historic period interpreted the friendship of Achilles and Patroclus in accordance with subsequently developed customs. The Homeric poems were the Bible of the Greeks, and formed the staple of their education; nor did they scruple to wrest the sense of the original, reading, like modern Bibliolaters, the sentiments and passions of a later age into the text. Of this process a good example is afforded by Æschines in the oration against Timarchus. While discussing this very question of the love of Achilles, he says: "He, indeed, conceals their love, and does not give its proper name to the affection between them, judging that the extremity of their fondness would be intelligible to instructed men among his audience." As an instance, the orator proceeds to quote the passage in which Achilles laments that he will not be able to fulfil his promise to Menœtius by bringing Patroclus home to Opus. He is here clearly introducing the sentiments of an Athenian hoplite who had taken the boy he loved to Syracuse and seen him slain there.

Homer stood in a double relation to the historical Greeks. On the one hand, he determined their development by the influence of his ideal characters. On the other, he underwent from them interpretations which varied with the spirit of each successive century. He created the national temperament, but received in turn the influx of new thoughts and emotions occurring in the course of its expansion. It is, therefore, highly important, on the threshold of this inquiry, to determine the nature of that Achilleian friendship to which the panegyrists and apologists of the custom make such frequent reference.

III.

The ideal of character in Homer was what the Greeks called heroic; what we should call chivalrous. Young men studied the *Iliad* as our ancestors studied the Arthurian romances, finding there a pattern of conduct raised almost too high above the realities of common life for imitation, yet stimulative of enthusiasm and exciting to the fancy. Foremost among the paragons of heroic virtue stood Achilles, the splendour of whose achievements in the Trojan war was only equalled by the pathos of his friendship. The love for slain Patroclus broke his mood of sullen anger, and converted his brooding sense of wrong into a lively thirst for vengeance. Hector, the slayer of Patroclus, had to be slain by Achilles, the comrade of Patroclus. No one can read the *Iliad* without observing that its action virtually turns upon the conquest which the passion of friendship gains over the passion of resentment in the breast of the chief actor. This the Greek students of Homer were not slow to see; and they not unnaturally selected the friendship of Achilles for their ideal of manly love. It was a powerful and masculine emotion, in which effeminacy had no part, and which by no means excluded the ordinary sexual feelings. Companionship in battle and the chase, in public and in private affairs of life, was the communion proposed by Achilleian friends--not luxury or the delights which feminine attractions offered. The tie was both more spiritual and more energetic than that which bound man to woman. Such was the type of comradeship delineated by Homer; and such, in spite of the modifications suggested by later poets, was the conception retained by the Greeks of this heroic friendship. Even Æschines, in the place above quoted, lays stress upon the mutual loyalty of Achilles and Patroclus as the strongest bond of their affection: "regarding, I suppose, their loyalty and mutual goodwill as the most touching feature of their love." [1]

Footnotes

3:1 Compare the fine rhetorical passage in Max. Tyr., *Dissert.*, xxiv. 8, ed. Didot, 1842.

IV.

Thus the tale of Achilles and Patroclus sanctioned among the Greeks a form of masculine love, which, though afterwards connected with paiderastia properly so called, we are justified in describing as heroic, and in regarding as one of the highest products of their emotional life. It will be seen, when we come to deal with the historical manifestations of this passion, that the heroic love which took its name from Homer's Achilles existed as an ideal rather than an actual reality. This, however, is equally the case with Christianity and chivalry. The facts of feudal history fall below the high conception which hovered like a dream above the knights and ladies of the Middle Ages; nor has the spirit of the Gospel been realised, in fact, by the most Christian nations. Still we are not on that account debarred from speaking of both chivalry and Christianity as potent and effective forces.

V.

Homer, then, knew nothing of paiderastia, though the *Iliad* contained the first and noblest legend of heroic friendship. Very early, however, in Greek history boy-love, as a form of sensual passion, became a national institution. This is proved abundantly by mythological traditions of great antiquity, by legendary tales connected with the founding of Greek cities, and by the primitive customs of the Dorian tribes. The question remains how paiderastia originated among the Greeks, and whether it was introduced or indigenous.

The Greeks themselves speculated on this subject, but they arrived at no one definite conclusion. Herodotus asserts that the Persians learned the habit, in its vicious form, from the Greeks; 1 but, even supposing this assertion to be correct, we are not justified in assuming the same of all barbarians who were neighbours of the Greeks; since we know from the Jewish records and from Assyrian inscriptions that the Oriental nations were addicted to this as well as other species of sensuality. Moreover, it might with some strain on language be maintained that Herodotus, in the passage above referred to, did not allude to boy-love in general, but to the peculiarly Hellenic form of it which I shall afterwards attempt to characterise.

A prevalent opinion among the Greeks ascribed the origin of paiderastia to Crete; and it was here that the legend of Zeus and Ganymede was localised. 2 "The Cretans," says Plato; 3

"are always accused of having invented the story of Ganymede and Zeus, which is designed to justify themselves in the enjoyment of such pleasures by the practice of the god whom they believe to have been their lawgiver."

In another passage, 1 Plato speaks of the custom that prevailed before the time of Laius--in terms which show his detestation of a vice that had gone far toward corrupting Greek society. This sentence indicates the second theory of the later Greeks upon this topic. They thought that Laius, the father of Œdipus, was the first to practise *Hybris*, or lawless lust, in this form; by the rape committed on Chrysippus, the son of Pelops. 2 To this crime of Laius the Scholiast to the *Seven against Thebes* attributes all the evils which afterwards befell the royal house of Thebes, and Euripides made it the subject of a tragedy. In another but less prevalent Saga the introduction of paiderastia, is ascribed to Orpheus.

It is clear from these conflicting theories that the Greeks themselves had no trustworthy tradition on the subject. Nothing, therefore, but speculative conjecture is left for the modern investigator. If we need in such a matter to seek further than the primal instincts of human nature, we may suggest that, like the orgiastic rites of the later Hellenic cultus, paiderastia in its crudest form was transmitted to the Greeks from the East. Its prevalence in Crete, which, together with Cyprus, formed one of the principal links between Phœnicia and Hellas proper, favours this view. Paiderastia would, on this hypothesis like the worship of the Paphian and Corinthian Aphrodite, have to be regarded as in part an Oriental importation. ₃ Yet, if we adopt any such solution of the problem, we must not forget that in this, as in all similar cases, whatever the Greeks received from adjacent nations, they distinguished with the qualities of their own personality. Paiderastia in Hellas assumed Hellenic characteristics, and cannot be confounded with any merely Asiatic form of luxury. In the tenth section of this Essay I shall return to the problem, and advance my own conjecture as to the part played by the Dorians in the development of paiderastia into a custom.

It is enough for the present to remark that, however introduced, the vice of boy-love, as distinguished from heroic friendship, received religious sanction at an early period. The legend of the rape of Ganymede was invented, according to the passage recently quoted from Plato, by the Cretans with the express purpose of investing their pleasures with a show of piety. This localisation of the religious sanction of paiderastia in Crete confirms the hypothesis of Oriental influence; for one of the notable features of Græco-Asiatic worship was the consecration of sensuality in the Phallus cult, the *Hiero douloi* (temple slaves, or *bayadères*) of Aphrodite, and the eunuchs of the Phrygian mother. Homer tells the tale of Ganymede with the utmost simplicity. The boy was so beautiful that Zeus suffered him not to dwell on earth, but translated him to heaven, and appointed him the cupbearer of the immortals. The sensual desire which made the king of gods and men prefer Ganymede to Leda, Io, Danaë, and all the maidens whom he loved and left on earth, is an addition to the Homeric version of the myth. In course of time the tale of Ganymede, according to the Cretan reading, became the nucleus around which the paiderastic associations of the Greek race gathered, just as that of Achilles formed the main point in their tradition of heroic friendship. To the Romans and the modern nations the name of Ganymede, debased to Catamitus, supplied a term of reproach, which sufficiently indicates the nature of the love of which he became eventually the eponym.

Footnotes

4:1 i. 135.

4:2 Numerous localities, however, claimed this distinction. See Ath., xiii. 601. Chalkis in Eubœa, as well as Crete, could show the sacred spot where the mystical assumption of Ganymede was reported to have happened.

4:3 *Laws*, i. 636. Cp. *Timæus*, quoted by Ath., p. 602. Servius, *ad Aen.* x. 325, says that boy-love spread from Crete to Sparta, and thence through Hellas, and Strabo mentions its prevalence among the Cretans (x. 483). Plato (Rep. v. 452) speaks of the Cretans as introducing naked athletic sports.

5:1 *Laws*, viii. 863.

5:2 See Ath., xiii. 602. Plutarch, in the Life of Pelopidas (Clough, vol. ii, p. 219), argues against this view.

5:3 See Rosenbaum, *Lustseuche im Alterthume*, p. 118.

VI.

Resuming the results of the last four sections, we find two separate forms of masculine passion clearly marked in early Hellas--a noble and a base, a spiritual and a sensual. To the distinction between them the Greek conscience was acutely sensitive; and this distinction, in theory at least, subsisted throughout their history. They worshipped Erôs, as they worshipped Aphrodite, under the twofold titles of Ouranios (celestial) and Pandemos (vulgar, or *volvivaga*); and, while they regarded the one love with the highest approval, as the source of courage and greatness of soul, they never publicly approved the other. It is true, as will appear in the sequel of this essay, that boy-love in its grossest form was tolerated in historic Hellas with an indulgence which it never found in any Christian country, while heroic comradeship remained an ideal hard to realise, and scarcely possible beyond the limits of the strictest Dorian sect. Yet the language of philosophers, historians, poets and orators is unmistakable. All testify alike to the discrimination between vulgar and heroic love in the Greek mind. I purpose to devote a separate section of this inquiry to the investigation of these ethical distinctions. For the present, a quotation from one of the most eloquent of the later rhetoricians will sufficiently set forth the contrast, which the Greek race never wholly forgot: [1]--

"The one love is mad for pleasure; the other loves beauty. The one is an involuntary sickness; the other is a sought enthusiasm. The one tends to the good of the beloved; the other to the ruin of both. The one is virtuous; the other incontinent in all its acts. The one has its end in friendship; the other in hate. The one is freely given; the other is bought and sold. The one brings praise; the other blame. The one is Greek; the other is barbarous. The one is virile; the other effeminate. The one is firm and constant; the other light and variable. The man who loves the one love is a friend of God, a friend of law, fulfilled of modesty, and free of speech. He dares to court his friend in daylight, and rejoices in his love. He wrestles with him in the playground and runs with him in the race, goes afield with him to the hunt, and in battle fights for glory at his side. In his misfortune he suffers, and at his death he dies with him. He needs no gloom of night, no desert place, for this society. The other lover is a foe to heaven, for he is out of tune and criminal; a foe to law, for he transgresses law. Cowardly, despairing, shameless, haunting the dusk, lurking in desert places and secret dens, he would fain be never seen consorting with his friend, but shuns the light of day, and follows after night and darkness, which the shepherd hates, but the thief loves."

And again, in the same dissertation, Maximus Tyrius speaks to like purpose, clothing his precepts in imagery:--

"You see a fair body in bloom and full of promise of fruit. Spoil not, defile not, touch not the blossom. Praise it, as some wayfarer may praise a plant-even so by Phœbus' altar have I seen a young palm shooting toward the sun. Refrain from Zeus' and Phœbus? tree; wait for the fruit-season, and thou shalt love more righteously."

With the baser form of paiderastia I shall have little to do in this essay. Vice of this kind does not vary to any great extent, whether we observe it in Athens or in Rome, in Florence of the sixteenth or in Paris of the nineteenth century; [2] nor in Hellas was it more noticeable than elsewhere, except for its comparative publicity. The nobler type of masculine love developed by the Greeks is, on the contrary, almost unique [3] in the history of the human race. It is that which more than anything else distinguishes, the

Greeks from the barbarians of their own time, from the Romans, and from modern men in all that appertains to the emotions. The immediate subject of the ensuing inquiry will, therefore, be that mixed form of paiderastia upon which the Greeks prided themselves, which had for its heroic ideal the friendship of Achilles and Patroclus, but which in historic times exhibited a sensuality unknown to Homer. ₁ In treating of this unique product of their civilisation I shall use the terms *Greek Love*, understanding thereby a passionate and enthusiastic attachment subsisting between man and youth, recognised by society and protected by opinion, which, though it was not free from sensuality, did not degenerate into mere licentiousness.

Footnotes

7:1 Max. Tyr., *Dissert.*, ix.

7:2 See Sismondi, vol. ii. p. 324; Symonds, *Renaissance in Italy*, *Age of the Despots*, p. 435; Tardieu, *Attentats aux Mœurs*, *Les Ordures de Paris*; Sir R. Burton's *Terminal Essay* to the "Arabian Nights"; Carlier, Les Deux Prostitutions, etc.

7:3 I say almost, because something of the same sort appeared in Persia at the time of Saadi.

8:1 Plato, in the *Phœdrus*, the *Symposium*, and the *Laws*, is decisive on the mixed nature of paiderastia.

VII.

Before reviewing the authors who deal with this subject in detail, or discussing the customs of the several Greek states, it will be well to illustrate in general the nature of this love, and to collect the principal legends and historic tales which set it forth.

Greek love was, in its origin and essence, military. Fire and valour, rather than tenderness or tears, were the external outcome of this passion; nor had *Malachia*, effeminacy, a place in its vocabulary. At the same time it was exceedingly absorbing. "Half my life," says the lover, "lives in thine image, and the rest is lost. When thou art kind, I spend the day like a god; when thy face is turned aside, it is very dark with me." 2 Plato, in his celebrated description of a lover's soul, writes 3:--

"Wherever she thinks that she will behold the beautiful one, thither in her desire she runs. And when she has seen him, and bathed herself with the waters of desire, her constraint is loosened and she is refreshed, and has no more pangs and pains; and this is the sweetest of all pleasures at the time, and is the reason why the soul of the lover will never forsake his beautiful one, whom he esteems above all; he has forgotten mother and brethren and companions, and he thinks nothing of the neglect and loss of his property. The rules and proprieties of life, on which he formerly prided himself, he now despises, and is ready to sleep like a servant, wherever he is allowed, as near as he can to his beautiful one, who is not only the object of his worship, but the only physician who can heal him in his extreme agony."

These passages show how real and vital was the passion of Greek love. It would be difficult to find more intense expressions of affection in modern literature. The effect produced upon the lover by the presence of his beloved was similar to that inspiration which the knight of romance received from his lady.

"I know not," says Phædrus, in the *Symposium* of Plato, 1" any greater blessing to a young man beginning life than a virtuous lover, or to the lover than a beloved youth. For the principle which ought to be the guide of men who would nobly live--that principle, I say, neither kindred, nor honour, nor wealth, nor any other motive is able to implant so well as love. Of what am, I speaking? Of the sense of honour and dishonour, without which neither states nor individuals ever do any good or great work. And I say that a lover who is detected in doing any dishonourable act, or submitting, through cowardice, when any dishonour is done to him by another, will be more pained at being detected by his beloved than at being seen by his father, or by his companions, or by any one else. The beloved, too, when he is seen in any disgraceful situation, has the same feeling about his lover. And if there were only some way of contriving that a state or an army should be made up of lovers and their loves, they would be the very best governors of their own city, abstaining from all dishonour; and emulating one another in honour; and when fighting at one another's side, although a mere handful, they would overcome the world. For what lover would not choose rather to be seen by all mankind than by his beloved, either when abandoning his post, or throwing away his arms? He would be ready to die a thousand deaths rather than endure this. Or who would desert his beloved or fail him in the hour of danger? The veriest coward would become an inspired hero, equal to the bravest, at such a time; love would inspire him. That courage which, as Homer says, the god breathes into the soul of heroes, love of his own nature inspires into the lover."

With the whole of this quotation we might compare what Plutarch in the Life of Pelopidas relates about the composition of the Sacred Band; 2 while the following anecdote from the *Anabasis* of Xenophon may serve to illustrate the theory that regiments should consist of lovers. 3 Episthenes of Olynthus, one of Xenophon's hoplites, saved a beautiful boy from the slaughter commanded by Seuthes in a Thracian village. The king could not understand why his orders had not been obeyed, till Xenophon excused his hoplite by explaining that Episthenes was a passionate boy-lover, and that he had once formed a corps of none but beautiful men. Then Seuthes asked Episthenes if he was willing to die instead of the boy, and he answered, stretching out his neck, "Strike," he says, "if the boy says 'Yes,' [4] and will be pleased with it." At the end of the affair, which is told by Xenophon with a quiet humour that brings a little scene of Greek military life vividly before us, Seuthes gave the boy his liberty, and the soldier walked away with him.

In order further to illustrate the hardy nature of Greek love I may allude to the speech of Pausanias in the *Symposium* of Plato. [1] The fruits of love, he says, are courage in the face of danger, intolerance of despotism, the virtues of the generous and haughty soul.

"In Ionia," he adds, "and other places, and generally in countries which are subject to the barbarians, the custom is held to be dishonourable; loves of youths share the evil repute of philosophy and gymnastics because they are inimical to tyranny, for the interests of rulers require that their subjects should be poor in spirit, and that there should be no strong bond of friendship or society among them, which love, above all other motives, is likely to inspire, as our Athenian tyrants learned by experience."

Footnotes

8:2 Theocr., *Paidika*, probably an Æolic poem of much older date.

8:3 *Phædrus*, p. 252. Jowett's translation.

9:1 Page 178, Jowett.

9:2 Clough, vol. ii. p. 218.

9:3 Book vii. 4, 7.

9:4 We may compare a passage from the *Symposium* ascribed to Xenophon VIII. 32.

VIII.

Among the myths to which Greek lovers referred with pride, besides that of Achilles, were the legends of Theseus and Peirithous, of Orestes and Pylades, of Talos and Rhadamanthus, of Damon and Pythias. Nearly all the Greek gods, except, I think, oddly enough, Ares, were famous for their love. Poseidon, according to Pindar, loved Pelops; Zeus, besides Ganymede, was said to have carried off Chrysippus. Apollo loved Hyacinth, and numbered among his favourites Branchos and Claros. Pan loved Cyparissus, and the spirit of the evening star loved Hymenæus. Hypnos, the God of slumber, loved Endymion, and sent him to sleep with open eyes, in order that he might always gaze upon their beauty. (Ath. xiii. 564). The myths of Phœbus, Pan, and Hesperus, it may be said in passing, are paiderastic parallels to the tales of Adonis and Daphine. They do not represent the specific quality of national Greek love at all in the same way as the legends of Achilles, Theseus, Pylades, and Pythias. We find in them merely a beautiful and romantic play of the mythopœic fancy, after paiderastic had taken hold on the imagination of the race. The case is different with Herakles, the patron, eponym, and ancestor of Dorian Hellas. He was a boy-lover of the true heroic type. In the innumerable amours ascribed to him we always discern the note of martial comradeship. His passion for Iolaus was so famous that lovers swore their oaths upon the Theban's tomb; [2] while the story of his loss of Hylas supplied Greek poets with one of their most charming subjects. From the idyll of Theocritus called *Hylas* we learn some details about the relation between lover and beloved, according to the heroic ideal.

"Nay, but the son of Amphitryon, that heart of bronze, he that abode the wild lion's onset, loved a lad, beautiful Hylas--Hylas of the braided locks, and he taught him all things as a father teaches his child, all whereby himself became a mighty man and renowned in minstrelsy. Never was he apart from Hylas,.... and all this that the lad might be fashioned to his mind, and might drive a straight furrow, and come to the true measure of man." [1]

Footnotes

10:1 Page 182, Jowett.

10:2 Plutarch, *Eroticus*, cap. xvii. p. 761, 40, Reiske.

11:1 Lang's translation, p. 63.

IX.

Passing from myth to semi-legendary history, we find frequent mention made of lovers in connection with the great achievements of the earliest age of Hellas. What Pausanias and Phædrus are reported to have said in the *Symposium* of Plato, is fully borne out by the records of the numerous tyrannicides and self-devoted patriots who helped to establish the liberties of the Greek cities. When Epimenides of Crete required a human victim in his purification of Athens from the *Musos* of the Megacleidæ, two lovers, Cratinus and Aristodemus, offered themselves as a voluntary sacrifice for the city. 2 The youth died to propitiate the gods; the lover refused to live without him. Chariton and Melanippus, who attempted to assassinate Phalaris of Agrigentum, were lovers. 3 So were Diocles and Philolaus, natives of Corinth, who removed to Thebes, and after giving laws to their adopted city, died and were buried in one grave. 4 Not less celebrated was another Diocles, the Athenian exile, who fell near Megara in battle, fighting for the boy he loved. 5 His tomb was honoured with the rites and sacrifices specially reserved for heroes. A similar story is told of the Thessalian horseman Cleomachus. 6 This soldier rode into a battle which was being fought between the people of Eretria and Chalkis, inflamed with such enthusiasm for the youth he beloved, that he broke the foemen's ranks and won the victory for the Chalkidians. After the fight was over Cleomachus was found among the slain, but his corpse was nobly buried; and from that time forward love was honoured by the men of Chalkis. These stories might be paralleled from actual Greek history. Plutarch, commenting upon the courage of the sacred band of Thebans, 7 tells of a man "who, when his enemy was going to kill him, earnestly requested him to run him through the breast, that his lover might not blush to see him wounded in the back." In order to illustrate the haughty temper of Greek lovers, the same author, in his *Erotic Dialogue*, records the names of Antileon of Metapontum, who braved a tyrant in the cause of a boy he loved; 1 of Crateas, who punished Archelaus with death for an insult offered to him; of Pytholaus, who treated Alexander of Pheræ in like manner; and of another youth who killed the Ambracian tyrant Periander for a similar affront. 2 To these tales we might add another told by Plutarch in his Life of Demetrius Poliorketes. This man insulted a boy called Damocles, who, finding no other way to save his honour, jumped into a cauldron of boiling water and was killed upon the spot. 3 A curious legend belonging to semi-mythical romance related by Pausanias, 4 deserves a place here, since it proves to what extent the popular imagination was impregnated by notions of Greek love. The city of Thespia was at one time infested by a dragon, and young men were offered to appease its fury every year. They all died unnamed and unremembered except one, Cleostratus. To clothe this youth, his lover, Menestratus, forged a brazen coat of mail, thick set with hooks turned upwards. The dragon swallowed Cleostratus and killed him, but died by reason of the hooks. Thus love was the salvation of the city and the source of immortality to the two friends.

It would not be difficult to multiply romances of this kind the rhetoricians and moralists of later Greece abound in them. ₅ But the most famous of all remains to be recorded. This is the story of Harmodius and Aristogeiton, who freed Athens from the tyrant Hipparchus. There is not a speech, a poem, an essay, a panegyrical oration in praise of either Athenian liberty or Greek love which does not tell the tale of this heroic friendship. Herodotus and Thucydides treat the event as matter of serious history. Plato refers to it as the beginning of freedom for the Athenians. "The drinking-song in honour of these lovers is one of the most precious fragments of popular Greek poetry which we possess. As in the cases of Lucretia and Virginia, so here a tyrant's intemperance was the occasion, if not the cause, of a great nation's rising. Harmodius and Aristogeiton were reverenced as martyrs and saviours of their country. Their names gave consecration to the love which made them bold against the despot, and they became at Athens eponyms of "paiderastia." ₁

Footnotes

11:2 See Athenæus, xiii. 602, for the details.

11:3 See Athenæus, xiii. 602, who reports an oracle in praise of these lovers.

11:4 Ar., *Pol.*, ii. 9.

11:5 See Theocr., *Aites* and the *Scholia*.

11:6 See Plutarch's *Eroticus*, 760, 42, where the story is reported on the faith of Aristotle.

11:7 *Pelopidas*, Clough's trans., vol. ii. p. 218.

12:1 Cap. xvi. p. 760, 21.

12:2 Cap. xxiii. p. 768, 53. Compare Max. Tyr., *Dissert.*, xxiv. i. See, too, the chapter on Tyrannicide in Ar. Pol., viii. (v.) 10.

12:3 Clough's trans., vol. v. p. 118.

12:4 *Hellenics*, bk. ix. cap. xxvi.

12:5 Suidas, under the heading *Paidika*, tells of two lovers who both died in battle, fighting each to save the other.

X.

A considerable majority of the legends which have been related in the preceding section are Dorian, and the Dorians gave the earliest and most marked encouragement to Greek love. Nowhere else, indeed, except among the Dorians, who were an essentially military race, living like an army of occupation in the countries they had seized, herding together in barracks and at public messes, and submitting to martial drill and discipline, do we meet with paiderastia developed as an institution. In Crete and Lacedæmon it became a potent instrument of education. What I have to say, in the first instance on this matter is derived almost entirely from C. O. Müller's *Dorians*, [2] to which work I refer my readers for the authorities cited in illustration of each detail. Plato says that the law of Lycurgus in respect to love was *Poikiles*, [3] by which he means that it allowed the custom under certain restrictions. It would appear that the lover was called Inspirer, at Sparta, while the youth he loved was named Hearer. These local phrases sufficiently indicate the relation which subsisted between the pair. The lover taught, the hearer learned; and so from man to man was handed down the tradition of heroism, the peculiar tone and temper of the state to which, in particular among the Greeks, the Dorians clung with obstinate pertinacity. Xenophon distinctly states that love was maintained among the Spartans with a view to education; and when we consider the customs of the state, by which boys were separated early from their homes and the influences of the family were almost wholly wanting, it is not difficult to understand the importance of the paiderastic institution. The Lacedæmonian lover might represent his friend in the Assembly. He was answerable for his good conduct, and stood before him as a pattern of manliness, courage, and prudence. Of the nature of his teaching we may form some notion from the precepts addressed by the Megarian Theognis to the youth Kurnus. In battle the lovers fought side by side, and it is worthy of notice that before entering into an engagement the Spartans sacrificed to Erôs. It was reckoned a disgrace if a youth found no man to be his lover. Consequently we find that the most illustrious Spartans are mentioned by their biographers in connection with their comrades. Agesilaus heard Lysander; Archidamus, his son loved Cleonymus; Cleomenes III. was the hearer of Xenares and the inspirer of Panteus. The affection of Pausanias, on the other hand, for the boy Argilus, who betrayed him according to the account of Thucydides, [1] must not be reckoned among these nobler loves. In order to regulate the moral conduct of both parties, Lycurgus made it felony, punishable with death or exile, for the lover to desire the person of a boy in lust; and, on the other hand, it was accounted exceedingly disgraceful for the younger to meet the advances of the elder with a view to gain. Honest affection and manly self-respect were exacted on both sides; the bond of union implied no more of sensuality than subsists between a father and a son, a brother and a brother. At the same time great license of intercourse was permitted. Cicero, writing long after the great age of Greece, but relying probably upon sources to which we have no access, asserts that "Lacedæmonii ipsi cum omnia concedunt in amore juvenum *præter stuprum* tenui sane muro dissæpiunt id quod excipiunt: *complexus enim concubitusque permittunt.*" 2"The Lacedemonians, while they permit all things except outrage in the love of youths, certainly distinguish the forbidden by a thin wall of partition from the sanctioned, for they allow embraces and a common couch to lovers."

In Crete the paiderastic institutions were even more elaborate than at Sparta. The lover was called *Philetor*, and the beloved one *Kleinos*. When a man wished to attach to himself a youth in the recognised bonds of friendship, he took him away from his home, with a pretence of force, but not without the connivance, in most cases, of his friends. 3 For two months the pair lived together among the hills, hunting and fishing. Then the Philetor gave gifts to the youth, and suffered him to return to his relatives, If the Kleinos (illustrious or laudable) had received insult or ill-treatment during the probationary weeks, he now could get redress at law. If he was satisfied with the conduct of his would-be comrade, he changed his title from *Kleinos* to *Parastates* (comrade and bystander in the ranks of battle and life), returned to the Philetor, and lived thenceforward in close bonds of public intimacy with him.

The primitive simplicity and regularity of these customs make it appear strange to modern minds; nor is it easy to understand how they should ever have been wholly free from blame. Yet we must remember the influences which prevalent opinion and ancient tradition both contribute toward preserving a delicate sense of honour under circumstances of apparent difficulty. The careful reading of one Life by Plutarch, that, for instance, of Cleomenes or that of Agis, will have more effect in presenting the realities of Dorian existence to our imagination than any amount of speculative disquisition. Moreover, a Dorian was exposed to almost absolute publicity. He had no chance of hiding from his fellow-citizens the secrets of his private life. It was not, therefore, till the social and political complexion of the whole nation became corrupt that the institutions just described encouraged profligacy. 1 That the Spartans and the Cretans degenerated from their primitive ideal is manifest from the severe critiques of the philosophers. Plato, while passing a deliberate censure on the Cretans for the introduction of paiderastia into Greece, 2 remarks that *syssitia*, or meals in common, and *gymnasia* are favourable to the perversion of the passions. Aristotle, in a similar argument, 3 points out that the Dorian habits had a direct tendency to check the population by encouraging the love of boys and by separating women from the society of men. An obscure passage quoted from Hagnon by Athenæus might also be cited to prove that the Greeks at large had formed no high opinion of Spartan manners. 4 But the most convincing testimony is to be found in the Greek language: "to do like the Laconians, to have connection in Laconian way, to do like the Cretans," tell their own tale, especially when we compare these phrases with, "to do like the Corinthians, the

Lesbians, the Siphnians, the Phœnicians," and other verbs formed to indicate the vices localised in separate districts.

Up to this point I have been content to follow the notices of Dorian institutions which are scattered up and down the later Greek authors, and which have been collected by C. O. Müller.

I have not attempted to draw definite conclusions, or to speculate upon the influence which the Dorian section of the Hellenic family may have exercised in developing paiderastia. To do so now will be legitimate, always remembering that what we actually know about the Dorians is confined to the historic period, and that the tradition respecting their early customs is derived from second-hand authorities.

It has frequently occurred to my mind that the mixed type of paiderastia which I have named Greek Love took its origin in Doris. Homer, who knew nothing about the passion as it afterwards existed, drew a striking picture of masculine affection in Achilles. And Homer, I may add, was not a native of northern Greece. Whoever he was, or whoever they were, the poet, or the poets, we call Homer belonged to the south-east of the Ægean. Homer, then, may have been ignorant of paiderastia. Yet friendship occupies the first place in his hero's heart, while only the second is reserved for sexual emotion. Now Achilles came from Phthia, itself a portion of that mountain region to which Doris belonged. ₁ Is it unnatural to conjecture that the Dorians, in their migration to Lacedæmon and Crete, the recognised headquarters of the custom, carried a tradition of heroic paiderastia along with them? Is it unreasonable to surmise that here, if anywhere in Hellas, the custom existed from prehistoric times? If so, the circumstances of their invasion would have fostered the transformation of this tradition into a tribal institution. They went forth, a band of warriors and pirates, to cross the sea in boats, and to fight their way along the hills and plains of Southern Greece. The dominions they had conquered with their swords they occupied like soldiers. The camp became their country, and for a long period of time they literally lived upon the bivouac. Instead of a city-state, with its manifold complexities of social life, they were reduced to the narrow limits and the simple conditions of a roving horde. Without sufficiency of women, without the sanctities of established domestic life, inspired by the memory of Achilles, and venerating their ancestor Herakles, the Dorian warriors had special opportunity for elevating comradeship to the rank of an enthusiasm. The incidents of emigration into a distant country-perils of the sea, passages of rivers and mountains, assaults of fortresses and cities, landings on a hostile shore, night-vigils by the side of blazing beacons, foragings for food, picquet services in the front of watchful foes-involved adventures capable of shedding the lustre of romance on friendship. These circumstances, by bringing the virtues of sympathy with the weak, tenderness for the beautiful, protection for the young, together with corresponding qualities of gratitude, self-devotion and admiring attachment, into play, may have tended to cement unions between man and man no less firm than that of marriage. On such connections a wise captain would have relied for giving strength to his battalion, and for keeping alive the flame of enterprise and daring. Fighting and foraging in company, sharing the same wayside board and heath-strewn bed, rallying to the comrade's voice in onset, relying on the comrade's shield when fallen, these men learned the meanings of the words *Philetor* and *Parastates*. To be loved was honourable, for it implied being worthy to be died for. To love was glorious, since it pledged the lover to self-sacrifice in case of need. In these conditions the paiderastic passion may have well combined manly virtue with carnal appetite, adding such romantic sentiment as some stern men reserve within their hearts for women. 1 A motto might be chosen for a lover of this early Dorian type from the Æolic poem ascribed to Theocritus: "And made me tender from the iron man I used to be."

In course of time, when the Dorians had settled down upon their conquered territories, and when the passions which had shown their more heroic aspect during a period of warfare came, in a period of idleness, to call for methods of restraint, then the discrimination between honourable and base forms of love, to which Plato pointed as a feature of the Dorian institutions, took place. It is also more than merely probable that in Crete, where these institutions were the most precisely regulated, the Dorian immigrants came into contact with Phœnician vices, the repression of which required the adoption of a strict code. 2 In this way paiderastia, considered as a mixed custom, partly martial, partly luxurious, recognised by public opinion and controlled by law, obtained among the Dorian Tribes, and spread from them throughout the states of Hellas. Relics of numerous semi-savage habits--thefts of food, ravishment as a prelude to marriage, and so forth--indicate in like manner the survival among the Dorians of primitive tribal institutions.

It will be seen that the conclusion to which I have been drawn by the foregoing considerations is that the mixed form of paiderastia called by me in this essay Greek love owed its peculiar quality, what Plato called its intricacy of "laws and customs," to two diverse strains of circumstances harmonised in the Greek temperament. Its military and enthusiastic elements were derived from the primitive conditions of the Dorians during their immigration into Southern Greece. Its refinements of sensuality and sanctified impurity are referable to contact with Phoenician civilisation. The specific form it assumed among the Dorians of the historic period, equally removed from military freedom and from Oriental luxury, can be ascribed to the operation of that organising, moulding and assimilating spirit which we recognise as Hellenic.

The position thus stated is, unfortunately, speculative rather than demonstrable; and in order to establish the reasonableness of the speculation, it would be natural at this point to introduce some account of paiderastia as it exists in various savage tribes, if their customs could be seen to illustrate the Doric phase of Greek love. This, however, is not the case. Study of Mr. Herbert Spencer's Tables, and of Bastian's *Der Mensch in der Geschichte* (vol. iii. pp. 304-323), together with the facts collected by travellers among the North American Indians, and the mass of curious information supplied by Rosenbaum in his *Geschichte der Lust-seuche im Alterthume*, makes it clear to my mind that the unisexual vices of barbarians follow, not the type of Greek paiderastia, but that of the Scythian disease of effeminacy, described by Herodotus and Hippocrates as something essentially foreign and non-Hellenic. In all these cases, whether we regard the Scythian impotent effeminates, the North American Bardashes, the Tsecats of Madagascar, the Cordaches of the Canadian Indians, and similar classes among Californian Indians, natives of Venezuela, and so forth--the characteristic point is that effeminate males renounce their sex, assume female clothes, and live either in promiscuous concubinage with the men of the tribe or else in marriage with chosen persons. This abandonment of the masculine attributes and habits, this assumption of feminine duties and costume, would have been abhorrent to the Doric custom. Precisely similar effeminacies were recognised as pathological by Herodotus, to whom Greek paiderastia was familiar. The distinctive feature of Dorian comradeship was that it remained on both sides masculine, tolerating no sort of softness. For similar reasons, what we know about the prevalence of sodomy among the primitive peoples of Mexico, Peru and Yucatan, and almost all half-savage nations, 1 throws little light upon the subject of the present inquiry. Nor do we gain anything of importance from the semi-religious practices of Japanese Bonzes or Egyptian priests. Such facts, taken in connection with abundant modern. experience of what are called unnatural vices, only prove the universality of unisexual indulgence in all parts of the world and under all conditions of society. Considerable psychological interest attaches to the study of these sexual aberrations. It is also true that we detect in them the germ or raw material of a custom which the Dorians moralised or developed after a specific fashion; but nowhere do we find an analogue to their peculiar institutions. It was just that effort to moralise and adapt to social use a practice which has elsewhere been excluded in the course of civil growth, or has been allowed to linger half-acknowledged as a remnant of more primitive conditions, or has re-appeared in the corruption of society; it was just this effort to elevate paiderastia according to the aesthetic standard of Greek ethics which constituted its distinctive quality in Hellas. We are obliged, in fact, to separate this, the true Hellenic manifestation of the paiderastic passion, from the effeminacies, brutalities and gross sensualities which can be noticed alike in imperfectly civilised and in luxuriously corrupt communities.

Before leaving this part of the subject, I must repeat that what I have suggested regarding the intervention of the Dorians in creating the type of Greek love is a pure speculation. If it has any value, that is due to the fixed and regulated forms which paiderastic institutions displayed at a very early date in Crete and Sparta, and also to the remnants of savage customs embedded in them. It depends to a certain extent also upon the absence of paiderastia in Homer. But on this point something still remains to be said. Our Attic authorities certainly regarded the Homeric poems as canonical books, decisive for the culture of the first stage of Hellenic history. Yet it is clear that Homer refined Greek mythology, while many of the cruder elements of that mythology survived from pre-Homeric times in local cults and popular religious observances. We know, moreover, that a body of non-Homeric writings, commonly called the cyclic poems, existed by the side of Homer, some of the material of which is preserved to us by dramatists, lyrics, historians, antiquaries and anecdotists. It is not impossible that this so-called cyclical literature contained paiderastic elements, which were eliminated, like the grosser forms of myth in the Homeric poems. 1 If this be conceded, we might be led to conjecture that paiderastia was a remnant of ancient savage habits, ignored by Homer, but preserved by tradition in the race. Given the habit, the Greeks were certainly capable of carrying it on without shame. We ought to resist the temptation to seek a high and noble origin for all Greek institutions. But there remains the fact that, however they acquired the habit, whether from North Dorian customs antecedent to Homer or from conditions of experience subsequent tot the Homeric age, the Greeks gave it a dignity and an emotional superiority which is absent in the annals of barbarian institutions. Instead of abandoning it as part of the obsolete lumber of their prehistoric origins, they chose to elaborate it into the region of romance and ideality. And this; they did in spite of Homer's ignorance of the passion or of his deliberate reticence. Whatever view, therefore, we may take about Homer's silence, and about the possibility of paiderastia occurring in lost poems of the cyclic type, or, lastly, about its probable survival in the people from an age of savagery, we are bound to regard its systematical development among the Dorians as a fact of paramount significance.

In that passage of the *Symposium* 2 where Plato notices the Spartan law of love as *Poikilos*, he speaks with disapprobation of the Bœotians, who were not restrained by custom and opinion within the same strict limits. Yet it should here be noted that the military aspect of Greek love in the historic period was nowhere more distinguished than at Thebes. Epaminsondas was a notable boy-lover; and the names of his beloved Asopichus and Cephisodorus, are mentioned by Plutarch. 3 They died, and were buried with him at Mantinea. The paiderastic legend of Herakles and Iolaus was localised in Bœotia; and the lovers, Diodes and Philolaus, who gave laws to Thebes, directly encouraged those masculine attachments, which had their origin in the Palæstra. 4 The practical outcome of these national institutions in the chief town of Bœotia was the formation of the so-called Sacred Band, or Band of Lovers, upon whom Pelopidas relied in his most perilous operations. Plutarch relates that they were enrolled, in the first instance, by Gorgidas, the rank and file of the regiment being composed of young men bound together by affection. Report goes that they were never beaten till the battle of Chæronea. At the end of that day, fatal to the liberties of Hellas, Philip of Macedon went forth to view the slain; and when he "came to that place where the three hundred that fought his phalanx lay dead together, he wondered, and understanding that it was the band of lovers, he shed tears, and said, 'Perish any man who suspects that these men either did or suffered anything that was base.'" [1] As at all the other turning-points of Greek history, so at this, too, there is something dramatic and eventful: Thebes was the last stronghold of Greek freedom; the Sacred Band contained the pith and flower of her army; these lovers had fallen to a man, like the Spartans of Leonidas at Thermopylæ, pierced by the lances of the Macedonian phalanx; then, when the day was over and the dead were silent, Philip, the victor in that fight, shed tears when he beheld their serried ranks, pronouncing himself therewith the fittest epitaph which could have been inscribed upon their stelë by a Hellene.

At Chæronea, Greek liberty, Greek heroism, and Greek love, properly so called, expired. It is not unworthy of notice that the son of the conqueror, young Alexander, endeavoured to revive the tradition of Achilleian friendship. This lad, born in the decay of Greek liberty, took conscious pleasure in enacting the part of a Homeric hero on the altered stage of Hellas and of Asia, with somewhat tawdry histrionic pomp. [2] Homer was his invariable companion upon his marches; in the Troad he paid special honour to the tomb of Achilles, running naked races round the barrow in honour of the hero, and expressing the envy which he felt for one who had so true a friend and so renowned a poet to record his deeds. The historians of his life relate that, while he was indifferent to women, [3] he was madly given to the love of males. This the story of his sorrow for Hephaistion sufficiently confirms. A kind of spiritual atavism moved the Macedonian conqueror to assume on the vast Bactrian plain the outward trappings of Achilles Agonistes. [4]

Returning from this digression upon Alexander's almost hysterical archaism, it should next be noticed that Plato includes the people of Elis in the censure which he passes upon the Bœotians. He accuses the Eleans of adopting customs which permitted youths to gratify their lovers without further distinction of age, or quality, or opportunity. In like manner Maximus Tyrius distinguishes between the customs of Crete and Elis: "While I find the laws of the Cretans excellent, I must condemn those of Elis for their license." [1] Elis, [2] like Megara, instituted a contest for beauty among youths; and it is significant that the Megarians were not uncommonly accused of *Hybris* or wanton lust, by Greek writers. Both the Eleans and the Megarians may therefore reasonably be considered to have exceeded the Greek standard of taste in the amount of sensual indulgence which they openly acknowledged. In Ionia and other regions of Hellas exposed to Oriental influences, Plato says that paiderastia was accounted a disgrace. [3] At the same time he couples with paiderastia in this place both addiction to gymnastic exercise and to philosophical studies, pointing out that despotism was always hostile to high thoughts and haughty customs. The meaning of the passage, therefore, seems to be that the true type of Greek love had no chance of unfolding itself freely on the shores of Asia Minor. Of paiderastic *Malakia*, or effeminacy, there is here no question, else Plato would probably have made Pausanias use other language.

Footnotes

13:1 See, for example, *Æschines against Timarchus*, 59.

13:2 Trans. by Sir G. C. Lewis, vol. ii. pp. 306-313.

13:3 *Symp.* 182 A.

14:1 i. 132.

14:2 *De Rep.*, iv. 4.

14:3 I need hardly point out the parallel between this custom and the marriage customs of half-civilised communities.

15:1 The general opinion of the Greeks with regard to the best type of Dorian love is well expressed by Maximus Tyrius, *Dissert.*, xxvi. 8. "It is esteemed a disgrace to a Cretan youth to have no lover. It is a disgrace for a Cretan youth to tamper with the boy he loves. O custom, beautifully blent of self-restraint and passion! The man of Sparta loves the lad of Lacedæmon, but loves him only as one loves a fair statue; and many love one, and one loves many."

15:2 *Laws*, i. 636.

15:3 *Pol*, ii. 7, 4.

15:4 Lib. 13,602, E.

16:1 It is not unimportant to note in this connection that paiderastia of no ignoble type still prevails among the Albanian mountaineers.

17:1 The foregoing attempt to reconstruct a possible environment for the Dorian form of paiderastia is, of course, wholly imaginative. Yet it receives certain support from what we know about the manners of the Albanian Mountaineers and the nomadic Tartar tribes. Aristotle remarks upon the Paiderastic customs of the Kelts, who in his times were immigrant.

17:2 See above, Section V.

19:1 It appears from the reports of travellers that this form of passion is not common among those African tribes who have not been corrupted by Mussulmans or Europeans.

20:1 It may be plausibly argued that Æschylus drew the subject of his *Myrmidones* from some such non-Homeric epic. See below, Section XII.

20:2 182 A.. Cp. Laws, i. 636.

20:3 Eroticus, xvii. p. 761, 34

20:4 See Plutarch, *Pelopidas*. Clough, vol. ii. p. 2 19.

21:1 Clough, as quoted above, p. 219.

21:2 The connection of the royal family of Macedon by descent with the Æacidæ, and the early settlement of the Dorians in Macedonia, are noticeable.

21:3 Cf. Athenæus, x. 435.

21:4 Hadrian in Rome, at a later period, revived the Greek tradition, with even more of caricature. His military ardour, patronage of art, and for Antinous seem to hang together.

22:1 *Dissert.*, xxvi. 8.

22:2 See Athen., xiii. 609, F. The prize was armour and the wreath of myrtle.

22:3 *Symp.* 182, B. In the *Laws*, however, he mentions the Barbarians as corrupting Greek morality in this respect. We have here a further proof that it was the noble type of love which the Barbarians discouraged. For *Malakia* they had no dislike.

XI.

Before proceeding to discuss the conditions under which paiderastia existed in Athens, it may be well to pause and to consider the tone adopted with regard to it by some of the earlier Greek poets. Much that is interesting on the subject of the true Hellenic Erôs can be gathered from Theognis, Solon, Pindar, Æschylus, and Sophocles; while the lyrics of Anacreon, Alcæus, Ibycus, and others of the same period illustrate the wanton and illiberal passion (*Hybris*) which tended to corrode and undermine the nobler feeling.

It is well-known that Theognis and his friend Kurnus were members of the aristocracy of Megara. After Megara had thrown off the yoke of Corinth in the early part of the sixth century, the city first submitted to the democratic despotism of Theagenes, and then for many years engaged in civil warfare. The large number of the elegies of Theognis are specially intended to instruct Kurnus how he ought to act as an illustrious party-leader of the nobles (*Esthloi*) in their contest with the people (*Deiloi*). They consist, therefore, of political and social precepts, and for our present purpose are only important as illustrating the educational authority assumed by a Dorian Philetor over his friend. The personal elegies intermingled with these poems on conduct reveal the very heart of a Greek lover at his early period. Here is one on loyalty:--

"Love me not with words alone, while your mind and thoughts are otherwise, if you really care for me and the heart within you is loyal. But love me with a pure and honest soul, or openly disown and hate me; let the breach between us be avowed. He who hath a single tongue and a double mind is a bad comrade, Kurnus, better as a foe than a friend." 1

The bitter-sweet of love is well described in the following couplets:--

"Harsh and sweet, alluring and repellent, until it be crowned with completion, is love for young men. If one brings it to perfection, then it is sweet; but if a man pursues and does not love, then it is of all things the most painful." 2

The same strain is repeated in the lines which begin, "a boy's love is fair to keep, fair to lay aside." 3 At one time Theognis tells his friend that he has the changeable temper of a hawk, the skittishness of a pampered colt.} 4 At another he remarks that boys are more constant than women in their affection. 5 His passion rises to its noblest height in a poem which deserves to rank with some of Shakespeare's sonnets, and which, like them, has fulfilled its own promise of immortality. 6 In order to appreciate the value of the fame conferred on Kurnus by Theognis and celebrated in such lofty strains, we must remember that these elegies were sung at banquets. "The fair young men," of whom the poet speaks, boy-lovers themselves, chaunted the praise of Kurnus to the sound of flutes, while the cups went round or the lyre was passed from hand to hand of merrymaking guests. A subject to which Theognis more than once refers is calumny:--

"Often will the folk speak vain things against thee in my ears, and against me in thine. Pay thou no heed to them." 1

Again, he frequently reminds the boy he loves, whether it be Kurnus or some other, that the bloom of youth is passing, and that this is a reason for showing kindness. 2 This argument is urged with what appears like coarseness in the following couplet:--

"O boy, so long as thy chin remains smooth, never will I cease from fawning, no, not if it is doomed for me to die." 3

A couplet, which is also attributed to Solon, shows that paiderastia at this time in Greece was associated with manly sports and pleasures:--

"Blest is the man who loves brave steeds of war,
Fair boys, and hounds, and stranger guests from far 4

Nor must the following be omitted:--

> "Blest is the man who loves, and after play,
> Whereby his limbs are supple made and strong,
> Retiring to his home, 'twixt sleep and song,
> Sports with a fair boy on his breast all day." 5

The following couplet is attributed to him by Plutarch, 6 nor does there seem any reason to doubt its genuineness. The text seems to be corrupt, but the meaning is pretty clear:--

"In the charming season of the flower-time of youth thou shalt love boys, yearning for their thighs and honeyed mouth."

Solon, it may be remembered, thought it wise to regulate the conditions under which the love of free youths might be tolerated.

The general impression produced by a careful reading of Theognis is that he entertained a genuine passion for Kurnus, and that he was anxious to train the young man's mind in what he judged the noblest principles. Love, at the same time, except in its more sensual moments, he describes as bitter-sweet and subject to anxiety. That perturbation of the emotions which is inseparable from any of the deeper forms of personal attachment, and which the necessary conditions of boy-love exasperated, was irksome to the Greek. It is not a little curious to observe how all the poets of the despotic age resent and fret against the force of their own feeling, differing herein from the singers of chivalry, who idealised the very pains of passion.

Of Ibycus, who was celebrated among the ancients as the lyrist of paiderastia, 1 very little has been preserved to us, but that little is sufficient to indicate the fervid and voluptuous style of his art. His imagery resembles that of Anacreon. The onset of love, for instance, in one fragment is compared to the down-swooping of a Thracian whirlwind; in another the poet trembles at the approach of Erôs like an old racehorse who is dragged forth to prove his speed once more.

Of the genuine Anacreon we possess more numerous and longer fragments, and the names of his favourites, Cleobulus, Smerdies, Leucaspis, are famous. The general tone of his love-poems is relaxed and Oriental, and his language abounds in phrases indicative of sensuality. The following may be selected:--

"Cleobulus I love, for Cleobulus I am mad, Cleobulus I watch and worship with my gaze." [2]

Again:--

"O boy, with the maiden's eyes, I seek and follow thee, but thou heedest not, nor knowest that thou art my soul's charioteer."

In another place he speaks of [3]--

"Love, the virginal, gleaming and radiant with desire."

Syneban (to pass the time of youth with friends) is a word which Anacreon may be said to have made current in Greek. It occurs twice in his fragments, [4] and exactly expresses the luxurious enjoyment of youthful grace and beauty which appear to have been his ideal of love. We are very far here from the Achilleian friendship of the *Iliad*. Yet occasionally Anacreon uses images of great force to describe the attack of passion, as when he says that love has smitten him with a huge axe and plunged him in a wintry torrent.--[5]

It must be remembered that both Anacreon and Ibycus were court poets, singing in the palaces of Polycrates and Hippias. The youths they celebrated were probably little better than the *exoleti* of a Roman Emperor. [6] This cannot be said exactly of Alcæus, whose love for black-eyed Lycus was remembered by Cicero and Horace. So little, however, is left of his erotic poems that no definite opinion can be formed about them. The authority of latter Greek authors justifies our placing him upon the list of those who helped to soften and emasculate the character of Greek love by their poems. [1]

Two Athenian drinking-songs preserved by Athenæus, [2] which seem to bear the stamp of the lyric age, may here be quoted. They serve to illustrate the kind of feeling to which expression was given in public by friends and boy-lovers--

"Would I were a lovely heap of ivory. and that lovely boys carried me into the Dionysian chorus." [3]

This is marked by a very delicate though naïf fancy. The next is no less eminent for its sustained, impassioned, simple, rhythmic feeling:--

"Drink with me, be young with me, love with me, wear crowns with me with me when I am mad be mad, with me when I am temperate be sober."

The greatest poet of the lyric age, the lyrist *par excellence* Pindar, adds much to our conception of Greek love at this period. Not only is the poem to Theoxenos, whom he loved, and in whose arms he is said to have died in the theatre at Argos, one of the most splendid achievements of his art; 4 but its choice of phrase, and the curious parallel which it draws between the free love of boys and the servile love of women, help us to comprehend the serious intensity of this passion. "The flashing rays of his forehead" and "is storm-tossed with desire," and "the young-limbed bloom of boys," are phrases which it is impossible adequately to translate. So, too, are the images by which the heart of him who does not feel the beauty of Theoxenos is said to have been forged with cold fire out of adamant, while the poet himself is compared to wax wasting under the sun's rays. In Pindar, passing from Ibycus and Anacreon, we ascend at once into a purer and more healthful atmosphere, fraught, indeed, with passion and pregnant with storm, but no longer simply sensual. Taken as a whole, the Odes of Pindar, composed for the most part in the honour of young men and boys, both beautiful and strong, are the work of a great moralist as well as a great artist. He never fails to teach by precept and example; he does not, as Ibycus is reported to have done, adorn his verse with legends of Ganymede and Tithonus, for the sake of insinuating compliments. Yet no one shared in fuller measure the Greek admiration for health and grace and vigour of limb. This is obvious in the many radiant pictures of masculine perfection he has drawn, as well as in the images by which he loves to bring the beauty-bloom of youth to mind. The true Hellenic spirit may be better studied in Pindar than in any other poet of his age; and after we have weighed his high morality, sound counsel, and reverence for all things good, together with the passion he avows, we shall have done something toward comprehending the inner nature of Greek love.

Footnotes

23:1 Bergk., *Poetæ Lyrica Græci*, vol. ii. p. 490, line 87 of Theognis.

23:2 *Ibid.*, line 1,353.

23:3 *Ibid.*, line 1,369.

23:4 *Ibid.*, lines 1,259-1,270.

23:5 *Ibid.*, line 1,267.

23:6 *Ibid.*, lines 237-254. Translated by me in *Vagabunduli Libellus*, p. 167.

24:1 Bergk., *Poetæ Lyrici Græci*, vol. ii. line 1,239.

24:2 *Ibid.*, line 1,304.

24:3 *Ibid.*, line 1,327.

24:4 *Ibid.*, line 1,253.

24:5 *Ibid.*, line 1,335.

24:6 *Eroticus*, cap. v. p. 751, 21. See Bergk., vol. ii. p. 430.

25:1 See Cic., *Tusc.*, iv. 33

25:2 Bergk., vol. iii. p. 1,013.

25:3 *Ibid.*, p. 1,045.

25:4 *Ibid.*, pp. 1,109, 1,023; fr. 24,46.

25:5 *Ibid.*, p. 1,023; fr. 48.

25:6 Maximus Tyrius *Dissert.*, xxvi., says that Smerdies was a Thracian, given, for his great beauty: by his Greek captors to Polycrates.

26:1 See what Agathon says in the *Thesmophoriazuse* of Aristophanes.

26:2 xv. 695.

26:3 Bergk., vol. iii. p. 1,293.

26:4 *Ibid.*, vol. i. p. 327.

XII.

The treatment of paiderastia upon the Attic stage requires separate considerations. Nothing proves the popular acceptance and national approval of Greek love more forcibly to modern minds than the fact that tragedians like Æschylus and Sophocles made it the subject of their dramas. From a notice in Athenæus it appears that Stesichorus, who first gave dramatic form to lyric poetry, composed interludes upon paiderastic subjects. 1 But of these it is impossible to speak, since their very titles have been lost. What immediately follows, in the narrative of Athenæus, will serve as text for what I have to say upon this topic. "And Aeschylus, that mighty poet, and Sophocles brought masculine loves into the theatre through their tragedies. Wherefore some are wont to call tragedy a paiderast; and the spectators welcome such." Nothing, unfortunately, remains of the plays which justified this language but a few fragments cited by Aristophanes, Plutarch, Lucian, and Athenæus. To examine these will be the business of this section.

The tragedy of the *Myrmidones*, which formed part of a trilogy by Æschylus upon the legend of Achilles, must have been popular at Athens, for Aristophanes quotes it no less than four times--twice in the *Frogs*, once in the *Birds*, and once in the *Ecclesiazusæ*. We can reconstruct its general plan from the lines which have come down to us on the authority of the writers above mentioned. 2 The play opened with an anapæstic speech of the chorus, composed of the clansmen of Achilles, who upbraided him for staying idle in his tent while the Achaians suffered at the hands of Hector. Achilles replied with the metaphor of the eagle stricken by an arrow winged from one of his own feathers. Then the embassy of Phoenix arrived, and Patroclus was sent forth to battle. Achilles, meanwhile, engaged in a game of dice; and while he was thus employed Antilochus entered with the news of the death of Patroclus. The next fragment brings the whole scene vividly before our eyes.

"Wail for me, Antilochus, rather than for the dead man--for me, Achilles, who still live." After this, the corpse of Patroclus was brought upon the stage, and the son of Peleus poured forth a lamentation over his friend. The *Threnos* of Achilles on this occasion was very celebrated among the ancients. One passage of unmeasured passion, which described the love which subsisted between the two heroes, has been quoted with varieties of reading by Lucian, Plutarch, and Athenæus. 1 Lucian says: "Achilles, bewailing the death of Patroclus with unhusbanded passion, broke forth into the truth in self-abandonment to woe." Athenæus gives the text as follows:--

"Hadst thou no reverence for the unsullied holiness of thighs, O thou ungrateful for the showers of kisses given."

What we have here chiefly to notice is the change which the tale of Achilles had undergone since Homer. 2 Homer represented Patroclus as older in years than the son of Peleus, but inferior to him in station; nor did he hint which of the friends was the *Erastes* of the other. That view of their comradeship had not occurred to him. Æschylus makes Achilles the lover; and for this distortion of the Homeric legend he was severely criticised by Plato. ₃ At the same time, as the two lines quoted from the *Threnos* prove, he treated their affection from the point of view of post-Homeric paiderastia.

Sophocles also wrote a play upon the legend of Achilles, which bears for its title *Achilles' Loves*. Very little is left of this drama; but Hesychius has preserved one phrase which illustrates the Greek notion that love was an effluence from the beloved person through the eyes into the lover's soul, ₁ while Stobæus quotes the beautiful simile by which love is compared to a piece of ice held in the hand by children. ₂ Another play of Sophocles, the *Niobe*, is alluded to by Plutarch and by Athenæus for the paiderastia which it contained. Plutarch's words are these: ₃ "When the children of Niobe, in Sophocles, are being pierced and dying, one of them cries out, appealing to no other rescuer or ally than his lover: Ho! comrade, up and aid me!" Finally, Athenæus quotes a single line from the *Colchian Women* of Sophocles, which alludes to Ganymede, and runs as follows: ₄ "Inflaming with his thighs the royalty of Zeus."

Whether Euripides treated paiderastia directly in any of his plays is not quite certain, though the title *Chrysippus* and one fragment preserved from that tragedy--

"Nature constrains me though I have sound judgment"--

justify us in believing that he made the crime of Laius his subject. It may be added that a passage in Cicero confirms this belief. ₅ The title of another tragedy, *Peirithous*, seems in like manner to point at friendship; while a beautiful quotation from the *Dictys* sufficiently indicates the high moral tone assumed by Euripides in treating of Greek love. It runs as follows:--"He was my friend; and never may love lead me to folly, nor to Kupris. There is, in truth, another kind of love--love for the soul, righteous, temperate., and good. Surely men ought to have made this law, that only the temperate and chaste should love, and send Kupris, daughter of Zeus, a-begging." The philosophic ideal of comradeship is here vitalised by the dramatic vigour of the poet; nor has the Hellenic conception of pure affection for "a soul, just, upright, temperate and good," been elsewhere more pithily expressed. The Euripidean conception of friendship, it may further be observed, is nobly personified in Pylades, who plays a generous and self-devoted part in the three tragedies of *Electra*, *Orestes*, and *Iphigenia in Tauris*.

Having collected these notices of tragedies which dealt with boy-love, it may be well to add a word upon comedies in the same relation. We hear of a *Paidika* by Sophron, a *Malthakoi* by the older Cratinus, a *Baptæe* by Empolis, in which Alcibiades and his society were satirised. *Paiderastes* is the title of plays by Diphilus and Antiphanes; *Ganymedes* of plays of Alkaeus, Antiphanes and Eubulus.

What has been quoted from Æschylus and Sophocles sufficiently establishes the fact that paiderastia was publicly received with approbation on the tragic stage. This should make us cautious in rejecting the stories which are told about the love adventures of Sophocles. ₁ Athenæus calls him a lover of lads, nor is it strange if, in the age of Pericles, and while he was producing the *Achilles' Loves*, he should have shared the tastes of which his race approved.

At this point it may be as well to mention a few illustrious names, which to the student of Greek art and literature are indissolubly connected with paiderastia. Parmenides, whose life, like that of Pythagoras, was accounted peculiarly holy, loved his pupil Zeno. ₂ Pheidias loved Pantarkes, a youth of Elis, and carved his portrait in the figure of a victorious athlete at the foot of the Olympian Zeus. ₃ Euripides is said to have loved the adult Agathon. Lysias, Demosthenes, and Æschines, orators whose conduct was open to the most searching censure of malicious criticism, did not scruple to avow their love. Socrates described his philosophy as the science of erotics. Plato defined the highest form of human existence to be "philosophy together with paiderastia," and composed the celebrated epigrams on Aster and on Agathon. This list might be indefinitely lengthened.

Footnotes

27:1 Athen., xiii. 601 A.

27:2 See the fragments of the *Myrmidones* in the *Poetæ Scenici Græci*. My interpretation of them is, of course, conjectural.

28:1 Lucian, Amores; Plutarch, Eroticus; Althenæus, xiii. 602 E.

28:2 Possibly Æschylus drew his fable from a non-Homeric source, but if so, it is curious that Plato should only refer to Homer.

28:3 *Symph.*, 180 A. Xenophon, *Symph.* 8, 31, points out that in Homer Achilles avenged the death of Patroclus, not as his lover, but as his comrade in arms.

29:1 Cf. Eurid., *Hippol.*, l. 525; Plato, *Phædr.*, p. 255; Max. Tyr., *Dissert.*, XXV. 2.

29:2 See *Poetæ Scenici, Fragments of Sophocles*.

29:3 *Eroticus*, p. 760 E.

29:4 Ath. p. 602 E.

29:5 *Tusc.*, iv. 33

30:1 See Athenæus, xiii. pp. 604, 605, for two very outspoken stories about Sophocles at Chios and apparently at Athens. In 582, e, he mentions one of the boys beloved by Sophocles; a certain Demophon.

30:2 Plato, *Parm.*, 127 A.

30:3 Pausanias, v. 11, and see Meier, p. 159, note 93.

XIII.

Before proceeding to collect some notes upon the state of paiderastia at Athens, I will recapitulate the points which I have already attempted to establish. In the first place, paiderastia was unknown to Homer. [4] Secondly, soon after the heroic age, two forms of paiderastia appeared in Greece--the one chivalrous and martial, which received a formal organisation in the Dorian states; the other sensual and lustful, which, though localised to some extent at Crete, pervaded the Greek cities like a vice. Of the distinction between these two loves the Greek conscience was well aware, though they came in course of time to be confounded. Thirdly, I traced the character of Greek love, using that term to indicate masculine affection of a permanent and enthusiastic temper, without further ethical qualification, in early Greek history and in the institutions of Dorians. In the fourth place, I showed what kind of treatment it received at the hands of the elegiac, lyric, and tragic poets.

It now remains to draw some picture of the social life of the Athenians in so far as paiderastia is concerned, and to prove how Plato was justified in describing Attic customs on this point as qualified by important restriction and distinction.

I do not know a better way of opening this inquiry, which must by its nature be fragmentary and disconnected, than by transcribing what Plato puts into the mouth of Pausanias in the Symposium. [1] After observing that the paiderastic customs of Elis and Bœotia involved no perplexity, inasmuch as all concessions to the god of love were tolerated, and that such customs did not exist in any despotic states, he proceeds to Athens.

"There is yet a more excellent way of legislating about them, which is our own way; but this, as I was saying, is rather perplexing. For observe that open loves are held to be more honourable than secret ones, and that the love of the noblest and highest, even if their persons are less beautiful than others, is especially honourable. Consider, too, how great is the encouragement which all the world gives to the lover; neither is he supposed to be doing anything dishonourable; but if he succeeds he is praised, and if he fail he is blamed. And in the pursuit of his love the custom of mankind allows him to do many strange things, which philosophy would bitterly censure if they were done from any motive of interest or wish for office or power. He may pray and entreat, and supplicate and swear, and be a servant of servants, and lie on a mat at the door; in any other case friends and enemies would be equally ready to prevent him, but now there is no friend who will be ashamed of him and admonish him, and no enemy will charge him with meanness or flattery; the actions of a lover have a grace which ennobles them, and custom has decided that they are highly, commendable, and that there is no loss of character in them; and, what is strangest of all, he only may swear or forswear himself (this is what the world says), and the gods will forgive his transgression, for there is no such thing as a lover's oath. Such is the entire liberty which gods and men have allowed the lover, according to the custom which prevails in our part of the world. From this point of view a man fairly argues that in Athens to love and to be loved is held to be a very honourable thing. But when there is another regime, and parents forbid their sons to talk with their lovers, and place them under a tutor's care, and their companions and equals cast in their teeth anything of this sort which they may observe, and their elders refuse to silence the reprovers, and do not rebuke them, any one who reflects on all this will, on the contrary, think that we hold these practices to be most disgraceful. But the truth, as I imagine, and as I said at first, is, that whether such practices are honourable or whether they are dishonourable is not a simple question; they are honourable to him who follows them honourably, dishonourable to him who follows them dishonourably. There is dishonour in yielding to the evil, or in an evil manner; but there is honour in yielding to the good, or in an honourable manner. Evil is the vulgar lover who loves the body rather than the soul, and who is inconstant because he is a lover of the inconstant, and, therefore, when the bloom of youth, which he was desiring, is over, takes wing and flies away, in spite of all his words and promises; whereas the love of the noble mind, which is one with the unchanging, is lifelong."

Pausanias then proceeds, at considerable length, to describe how the custom of Athens required deliberate choice and trial of character as a condition of honourable love; how it repudiated hasty and ephemeral attachments and engagements formed with the object of money-making or political aggrandisement; how love on both sides was bound to be disinterested, and what accession both of dignity and beauty the passion of friends obtained from the pursuit of philosophy and from the rendering of mutual services upon the path of virtuous conduct.

This sufficiently indicates, in general terms, the moral atmosphere in which Greek love flourished at Athens. In an earlier part of his speech Pausanias, after dwelling upon the distinction between the two kinds of Aphrodite, heavenly and vulgar, describes the latter in a way which proves that the love of boys was held to be ethically superior to that of women. [1]

"The Love who is the offspring of the common Aphrodite is essentially common, and has no discrimination, being such as the meaner sort of men feel, and is apt to be of women as well as of youths, and is of the body rather than the soul; the most foolish beings are the objects of this love, which desires only to gain an end, but never thinks of accomplishing the end nobly, and therefore does good and evil quite indiscriminately. The goddess who is his mother is far younger than the other, and she was born of the union of the male and female, and partakes of both."

Then he turns to the Uranian love.

"The offspring of the heavenly Aphrodite is derived from a mother in whose birth the female has no part. She is from the male only; this is that love which is of youths, and the goddess being older, has nothing of wantonness. Those who are inspired by this love turn to the male, and delight in him who is the most valiant and intelligent nature; any, one may recognise the pure enthusiasts in the very character of their attachments; for they love not boys, but intelligent beings whose reason is beginning to be developed, much about the time at which their beards begin to grow. And in choosing them as their companions they mean to be faithful to them, and pass their whole life in company with them, not to take them in their inexperience, and deceive them, and play the fool with them, or run away from one to another of them. But the love of young boys should be forbidden by law, because their future is uncertain; they may turn out good or bad, either in body or soul, and much noble enthusiasm may be thrown away upon them; in this matter the good are a law to themselves, and the coarser sort of lovers ought to be restrained by force, as we restrain or attempt to restrain them from fixing their affections on women of free birth."

These long quotations from a work accessible to every reader may require apology. My excuse for giving them must be that they express in pure Athenian diction a true Athenian view of this matter. The most salient characteristics of the whole speech are, first, the definition of a code of honour, distinguishing the nobler from the baser forms of paiderastia; secondly, the decided preference of male over female love; thirdly, the belief in the possibility of permanent affection between paiderastic friends; and, fourthly, the passing allusion to rules of domestic surveillance under which Athenian boys were placed. To the first of these points I shall have to return on another occasion. With regard to the second, it is sufficient for the present purpose to remember that free Athenian women were comparatively uneducated and uninteresting, and that the hetairai had proverbially bad manners. While men transacted business and enjoyed life in public, their wives and daughters stayed in the seclusion of the household, conversing to a great extent with slaves, and ignorant of nearly all that happened in the world around them. They were treated throughout their lives as minors by the law, nor could they dispose by will of more than the worth of a bushel of barley. It followed that marriages at Athens were usually matches of arrangement between the fathers of the bride and the bridegroom, and that the motives which induced a man to marry were less the desire for companionship than the natural wish for children and a sense of duty to the country. [1] Demosthenes, in his speech against Neæra, declares: [2] "We have courtesans for our pleasures, concubines for the requirements of the body, and wives for the procreation of lawful issue." If he had been speaking at a drinking-party, instead of before a jury, he might have added, "and young men for intellectual companions."

The fourth point which I have noted above requires more illustration, since its bearing on the general condition of Athenian society is important. Owing to the prevalence of paiderastia, a boy was exposed in Athens to dangers which are comparatively unknown in our great cities, and which rendered special supervision necessary. It was the custom for fathers, when they did not themselves accompany their sons, to commit them to the care of slaves chosen usually among the oldest and most trustworthy. The duty of the attendant guardian was not to instruct the boy, but to preserve him from the addresses of importunate lovers or from such assaults as Peisthetærus in the *Birds* of Aristophanes describes. [2] He followed his charge to the school and the gymnasium, and was responsible for bringing him home at the right hour. Thus at the end of the *Lysis* we read [3]:--

"Suddenly we were interrupted by the tutors of Lysis and Menexenus, who came upon us like an evil apparition with their brothers, and bade them go home, as it was getting late. At first, we and the bystanders drove them off; but afterwards, as they would not mind, and only went on shouting in their barbarous dialect, and got angry, and kept calling the boys--they appeared to us to have been drinking rather too much at the Hermæa, which made them difficult to manage--we fairly gave way and broke up the company."

In this way the daily conduct of Athenian boys of birth and good condition was subjected to observation; and it is not improbable that the charm which invested such lads as Plato portrayed in his *Charmides* and *Lysis* was partly due to the self-respect and self-restraint generated by the peculiar conditions under which they passed their life.

Of the way in which a Greek boy spent his day, we gain some notion from two passages in Aristophanes and Lucian. The Dikaios Logos [4] tells that--

"in his days, when justice flourished and self-control was held in honour, a boy's voice was never heard. He walked in order with his comrades of the same quarter, lightly clad even in winter, down to the school of the harp-player. There he learned old-fashioned hymns to the gods, and patriotic songs. While he sat, he took care to cover his person decently; and when he rose, he never forgot to rub out the marks which he might have left upon the dust lest any man should view them after he was gone.

At meals he ate what was put before him and refrained from idle chattering. Walking through the streets, he never tried to catch a passer's eye or to attract, a lover. He avoided the shops, the baths, 1 the Agora, the houses of Hetairai. 2 He reverenced old age and formed within his soul the image of modesty. In the gymnasium he indulged in fair and noble exercise, or ran races with his comrades among the olive-trees of the Academy."

The Adikos Logos replies by pleading that this temperate sort of life is quite old-fashioned; boys had better learn to use their tongues and bully. In the last resort he uses a clinching *argumentum ad juvenem*. 3

Were it nor for the beautiful and highly finished portraits in Plato, to which I have already alluded, the description of Aristophanes might be thought a mere ideal; and, indeed, it is probable that the actual life of the average Athenian boy lay mid-way between the courses prescribed by the Dikaios and the Adikos Logos.

Meanwhile, since Euripides, together with the whole school of studious and philosophic speculators, are aimed at in the speeches of the Adikos Logos, it will be fair to adduce a companion picture of the young Greek educated on the athletic system, as these men had learned to know him. I quote from the *Autolycus*, a satyric drama of Euripides:--

"There are a myriad bad things in Hellas, but nothing is worse than the athletes. To begin with, they do not know how to live like gentlemen, nor could they if they did; for how can a man, the slave of his jaws and his belly, increase the fortune left him by his father? Poverty and ill-luck find them equally incompetent. Having acquired no habits of good living, they are badly off when they come to roughing it. In youth they shine like statues stuck about the town, and take their walks abroad; but when old age draws nigh, you find them as threadbare as an old coat. Suppose a man has wrestled well, or runs fast, or has hurled a quoit, or given a black eye in fine style, has be done the state a service by the crowns he won? Do soldiers fight with quoits in hand, or without the press of shields can kicks expel the foeman from the ate? Nobody is fool enough to do these things with steel before his face. Keep, then, your laurels for the wise and good, for him who rules a city well, the just and temperate, who by his speeches wards off ill, allaying wars and civil strife. These are the things for cities, yea, and for all Greece to boast of."

Lucian represents, of course, a late period of Attic life. But his picture of the perfect boy completes, and in some points supplements, that of Aristophanes. Callicratidas, in the *Dialogue on Love*, has just drawn an unpleasing picture of a woman, surrounded in a fusty boudoir with her rouge-pots and cosmetics, perfumes, paints, combs, looking-glasses, hair dyes, and curling irons. Then he turns to praise boys. 1

"How different is a boy! In the morning he rises from his chaste couch, washes the sleep from his eyes with cold water, puts on his *chlamys*, 2 and takes his way to the school of the musician or the gymnast. His tutors and guardians attend him, and his eyes are bent upon the ground. He spends the morning in studying the poets and philosophers, in riding, or in military drill. Then he betakes himself to the wrestling-ground, and hardens his body with noontide heat and sweat and dust. The bath follows and a modest meal. After this he returns for awhile to study the lives of heroes and great men. After a frugal supper sleep at last is shed upon his eyelids."

Such is Lucian's sketch of the day spent by a young Greek at the famous University of Athens. Much is, undoubtedly, omitted; but enough is said to indicate the simple occupations to which an Athenian youth, capable of inspiring an enthusiastic affection, was addicted. Then follows a burst of rhetoric, which reveals, when we compare it with the dislike expressed for women, the deeply-seated virile nature of Greek love.

"Truly he is worthy to be loved. Who would not love Hermes in the palæstra, or Phœbus at the lyre, or Castor on the racing-ground? Who would not wish to sit face to face with such a youth, to hear him talk, to share his toils, to walk with him, to nurse him in sickness, to attend him on the sea, to suffer chains and darkness with him if need be? He who hated him should be my foe, and whoso loved him should be loved by me. At his death I would die; one grave should cover us both; one cruel hand cut short our lives!"

In the sequel of the dialogue Lucian makes it clear that he intends these raptures of Callicratidas to be taken in great measure for romantic boasting. Yet the fact remains that, till the last, Greek paiderastia among the better sort of men implied no effeminacy. Community of interest in sport, in exercise, and in open-air life rendered it attractive. [3]

"Sons of Eudiades, Euphorion,
After the boxing-match, in which he beat,
With wreaths I crowned, and set fine silk upon
His forehead and soft blossoms honey-sweet;

Then thrice I kissed him all beblooded there;
His mouth I kissed, his eyes, his every bruise
More fragrant far than frankincense, I swear,
Was the fierce chrism that from his brows did ooze."

"I do not care for curls or tresses
Displayed in wily wildernesses
I do not prize the arts that dye
A painted cheek with hues that fly:
Give me a boy whose face and hand
Are rough with dust or circus-sand,
Whose ruddy flesh exhales the scent
Of health without embellishment:
Sweet to my sense is such a youth,
Whose charms have all the charm of truth
Leave paints and perfumes, rouge, and curls,
To lazy, lewd Corinthian girls."

The palæstra was the place at Athens where lovers enjoyed the greatest freedom. In the *Phædrus* Plato observes that the attachment of the lover for a boy grew by meetings and personal contact 1 in the gymnasiums and other social resorts, and in the *Symposium* he mentions gymnastic exercises with philosophy, and paiderastia as the three pursuits of freemen most obnoxious to despots. Æschines, again describing the manners of boy-lovers in language familiar to his audience, uses these phrases: "having grown up in gymnasiums and games," and "the man having been a noisy haunter of gymnasiums, and having been the lover of multitudes." Aristophanes also in the *Wasps* 2 employs similar language: "and not seeking to go revelling around in exercising grounds." I may compare Lucian, *Amores*, cap. 2, "you care for gymnasiums and their sleek oiled combatants," which is said to a notorious boy-lover. Boys and men met together with considerable liberty in the porches, peristyles, and other adjuncts to an Attic wrestling-ground; and it was here, too, that sophists and philosophers established themselves with the certainty of attracting a large and eager audience for their discussions. It is true that an ancient law forbade the presence of adults in the wrestling-grounds of boys; but this law appears to have become almost wholly obsolete in the days of Plato. Socrates, for example, in the *Charmides*, goes down immediately after his arrival from the camp at Potidæa into the palæstra of Taureas to hear the news of the day, and the very first question which he asks his friends is whether a new beauty has appeared among the youths. 3 So again in the *Lysis*, Hippothales invites Socrates to enter the private palæstra of Miccus, where boys and men were exercising together on the feast-day of Hermes. 1 "The building," he remarks, "is a newly erected palæstra, and the entertainment is generally conversation, to which you are welcome." The scene which immediately follows is well known to Greek students as one of the most beautiful and vivid pictures of Athenian life. One group of youths are sacrificing to Hermes; another are casting dice in a corner of the dressing-room. Lysis himself is "standing among the other boys and youths, having a crown upon his head, like a fair vision, and not less worthy of praise for his goodness than for his beauty." The modesty of Lysis is shown by the shyness which prevents him joining Socrates' party until he has obtained the company of some of his young friends. Then a circle of boys and men, is formed in a corner of the court, and a conversation upon friendship begins. Hippothales, the lover of Lysis, keeps at a decorous distance in the background. Not less graceful as a picture is the opening of the Charmides. In answer to a question of Socrates, the frequenters of the palæstra tell him to expect the coming of young Charmides. He will then see the most beautiful boy in Athens at the time: "for those who are just entering are the advanced guard of the great beauty of the day, and he is likely to be not far off." There is a noise and a bustle at the door, and while the Socratic party continues talking Charmides enters. The effect produced is overpowering 2:--

"You know, my friend, that I cannot measure anything, and of the beautiful I am simply such a measure as a white line is of chalk; for almost all young persons appear to be beautiful in my eyes. But at that moment when I saw him coming in, I confess that I was quite astonished at his beauty and his stature; all the world seemed to be enamoured of him; amazement and confusion reigned when he entered; and a troop of lovers followed him. That grown-up men like ourselves should have been affected in this way was not surprising, but I observed that there was the same feeling among the boys; all of them, down to the very least child, turned and looked at him, as if he had been a statue."

Charmides, like Lysis, is persuaded to sit down by Socrates, who opens a discussion upon the appropriate question of *Sophrosyne*, or modest temperance and self-restraint. [3]

"He came as he was bidden, and sat down between Critias and me. Great amusement was occasioned by everyone pushing with might and main at hit; neighbour in order to make a place for him next to them, until at the two ends of the row one had to get up, and the other was rolled over sideways. Now I, my friend, was beginning to feel awkward; my former bold belief in my powers of conversing with him had vanished. And when Critias told him that I was the person who had the cure, he looked at me in such an indescribable manner, and was going to ask a question; and then all the people in the palæstra crowded about us, and, O rare! I caught a sight of the inwards of his garment, and took the flame. Then I could no longer contain myself. I thought how well Cydias understood the nature of love when, in speaking of a fair youth, he warns someone 'not to bring the fawn in the sight of the lion to be devoured by him,' for I felt that I had been overcome by a sort of wild-beast appetite."

The whole tenor of the dialogue makes it clear that, in spite of the admiration he excited, the honour paid him by a public character like Socrates, and the troops of lovers and of friends surrounding him, yet Charmides was unspoiled. His docility, modesty, simplicity, and healthiness of soul are at least as remarkable as the beauty for which he was so famous.

A similar impression is produced upon our minds by Autolycus in the *Symposium* of Xenophon. [1] Callias, his acknowledged lover, [2] had invited him to a banquet after a victory which he had gained in the pancration; and many other guests, including the Socratic party, were asked to meet him. Autolycus came, attended by his father; and as soon as the tables were covered and the seats had been arranged, a kind of divine awe fell upon the company. The grown-up men were dazzled by the beauty and the modest bearing of the boy, just as when a bright light is brought into a darkened room. Everybody gazed at him, and all were silent, sitting in uncomfortable attitudes of expectation and astonishment. The dinner party would have passed off very tamely if Phillipus, a professional diner-out and jester, had not opportunely made his appearance. Autolycus meanwhile never uttered a word, but lay beside his father like a breathing statue. Later on in the evening he was obliged to answer a question. He opened his lips with blushes, and all he said was, [3] "Not I, by gad." Still, even this created a great sensation in the company. Everybody, says Xenophon, was charmed to hear his voice and turned their eyes upon him. It should be remarked that the conversation at this party fell almost entirely upon matters of love. Critobulus, for example, who was very beautiful and rejoiced in having many lovers, gave a full account of his own feelings for Cleinias. [4]

"You all tell me," he argued, "that I am beautiful, and I cannot but believe you; but if I am, and if you feel what I feel when I look on Cleinias, I think that beauty is better worth having than all Persia. I would choose to be blind to everybody else if I could only see Cleinias, and I hate the night because it robs me of his sight. I would rather be the slave of Cleinias than live without him; I would rather toil and suffer danger for his sake than live alone at ease and in safety. I would go through fire with him, as you would with me. In my soul I carry an image of him better made than any sculptor could fashion."

What makes this speech the more singular is that Critobulus was a newly-married man.

But to return from this digression to the palæstra. The Greeks were conscious that gymnastic exercises tended to encourage, and confirm the habit of paiderastia. "The cities which have most to do with gymnastics," is the phrase which Plato uses to describe the states where Greek love flourished. 1 Herodotus says the barbarians borrowed gymnastics to ether with paiderastia from the Hellenes; and we hear that Polycrates of Samos caused the gymnasia to be destroyed when he wished to discountenance the love which lent the warmth of personal enthusiasm to political associations. 2 It was common to erect statues of love in the wrestling-grounds; and there, says Plutarch, 3 the god's wings grew so wide that no man could restrain his flight. Readers of the idyllic poets will remember that it was a statue of Love which fell from its pedestal in the swimming-bath upon the cruel boy who had insulted the body of his self-slain friend. 4 Charmus, the lover of Hippias, erected an image of Erôs in the academy at Athens which bore this epigram

"Love, god of many evils and various devices, Charmus set up this altar to thee upon the shady boundaries of the gymnasium." 5

Erôs, in fact, was as much at home in the gymnasia of Athens as Aphrodite in the temples of Corinth; he was the patron of paiderastia, as she of female love. Thus Meleager writes:--

"The Cyprian queen, a woman, hurls the fire that maddens men for females; but Erôs himself sways the love of males for males." 6

Plutarch, again, in the Erotic dialogue, alludes to "Erôs, where Aphrodite is not; Erôs apart from Aphrodite." These facts relating to the gymnasia justified Cicero in saying "Mihi quidem hæc in Græcorum gymnasiis nata consuetudo videtur: *in quibus isti liberi et concessi sunt amores*." He adds, with a true Roman's antipathy to Greek æsthetics and their flimsy screen for sensuality, "Bene ergo Ennius, *flagitii principium est nudare inter cives corpora*." 1 "To me, indeed, it seems that this custom was generated in the gymnasiums of the Greeks, for there those loves are freely indulged and sanctioned. Ennius therefore very properly observed that the beginning of vice is the habit of stripping the body among citizens."

The Attic gymnasia and schools were regulated by strict laws. We have already seen that adults were not supposed to enter the palæstra; and the penalty for the infringement of this rule by the gymnasiarch was death. In the same way schools had to be shut at sunset and not opened again before daybreak; nor was a grown-up man allowed to frequent them. The public chorus-teachers of boys were obliged to be above the age of forty. 2 Slaves who presumed to make advances to a free boy were subject to the severest penalties; in like manner they were prohibited from gymnastic exercises. Æschines, from whom we learn these facts, draws the correct conclusion that gymnastics and Greek love were intended to be the special privilege of freemen. Still, in spite of all restrictions, the palæstra was the centre of Athenian profligacy, the place in which not only honourable attachments were formed, but disgraceful bargains also were concluded; 3 and it is not improbable that men like Taureas and Miccus, who opened such places of amusement as a private speculation, may have played the part of go-betweens and panders. Their walls and the plane-trees which grew along their open courts were inscribed by lovers with the names of boys who had attracted them. To scrawl up, "Fair is Dinomeneus, fair is the boy," was a common custom, as we learn from Aristophanes and from this anonymous epigram in the *Anthology*: 4--

"I said and once again I said, 'fair, fair'; but still will I go on repeating how fascinating with his eyes is Dositheus. Not upon an oak, nor on a pine-tree, nor yet upon a wall, will I inscribe this word; but love is smouldering in my heart of hearts."

Another attention of the same kind from a lover to a boy was to have a vase or drinking-cup of baked clay made, with a portrait of the youth depicted on its surface, attended by winged genii of health and love. The word "Fair" was inscribed beneath, and symbols of games were added--a hoop or a fighting-cock. 1 Nor must I here omit the custom which induced lovers of a literary turn to praise their friends in prose or verse. Hippothales, in the *Lysis* of Plato, is ridiculed by his friends for recording the great deeds of the boy's ancestors, and deafening his ears with odes and sonnets. A diatribe on love, written by Lysias with a view to winning Phædrus, forms the starting-point of the dialogue between that youth and Socrates. 2 We have, besides, a curious panegyrical oration (called *Eroticos Logos*), falsely ascribed to Demosthenes, in honour of a youth, Epicrates, from which some information may be gathered concerning the topics usually developed in these compositions.

Presents were of course a common way of trying to win favour. It was reckoned shameful for boys to take money from their lovers, but fashion permitted them to accept gifts of quails and fighting cocks, pheasants, horses, dogs, and clothes. 3 There existed, therefore, at Athens frequent temptations for boys of wanton disposition, or for those who needed money to indulge expensive tastes. The speech of Æschines, from which I have already frequently quoted, affords a lively picture of the Greek rake's progress, in which Timarchus is described as having sold his person in order to gratify his gluttony and lust and love of gaming. The whole of this passage, 4 it may be observed in passing, reads like a description of Florentine manners in a sermon of Savonarola.

The shops of the barbers, surgeons, perfumers, and flower-sellers had an evil notoriety, and lads who frequented these resorts rendered themselves liable to suspicion. Thus Æschines accuses Timarchus of having exposed himself for hire in a surgeon's shop at the Peiræus; while one of Straton's most beautiful epigrams [5] describes an assignation which he made with a boy who had attracted his attention in a garland-weaver's stall. In a fragment from the *Pyraunos* of Alexis a young man declares that he found thirty professors of the "voluptuous life of pleasure," in the Cerameicus during a search of three days; while Cratinus and Theopompus might be quoted to prove the ill fame of the monument to Cimon and the hill of Lycabettus. [1]

The last step in the downward descent was when a youth abandoned the roof of his parents or guardians and accepted the hospitality of a lover. [2] If he did this, he was lost.

In connection with this portion of the subject it may be well to state that the Athenian law recognised contracts made between a man and boy, even if the latter where of free birth, whereby the one agreed to render up his person for a certain period and purpose, and the other to pay a fixed sum of money. [3] The phrase "a boy who has been a prostitute," occurs quite naturally in Aristophanes; [4] nor was it thought disreputable for men to engage in these *liaisons*. Disgrace only attached to the free youth who gained a living by prostitution; and he was liable, as we shall see, at law to loss of civil rights.

Public brothels for males were kept in Athens, from which the state derived a portion of its revenues. It was in one of these bad places that Socrates first saw Phædo. [5] This unfortunate youth was a native of Elis. Taken prisoner in war, he was sold in the public market to a slave-dealer, who then acquired the right by Attic law to prostitute his person and engross his earnings for his own pocket. A friend of Socrates, perhaps Cebes, bought him from his master, and he became one of the chief members of the Socratic circle. His name is given to the Platonic dialogue on immortality, and he lived to found what is called the Eleo-Socratic School. No reader of Plato forgets how the sage, on the eve of his death, stroked the beautiful long hair of Phædo, [6] and prophesied that he would soon have to cut it short in mourning for his teacher.

Agathocles, the tyrant of Syracuse, is said to have spent his youth in brothels of this sort-by inclination, however, if the reports of his biographers be not calumnious.

From what has been collected on this topic, it will be understood that boys in Athens not unfrequently caused quarrels and street-brawls, and that cases for recovery of damages or breach of contract were brought before the Attic law-courts. The Peiræus was especially noted for such scenes of violence. The oration of Lysias against Simon is a notable example of the pleadings in a cause of this description. ₁Simon the defendant and Lysias the plaintiff (or some one for whom Lysias had composed the speech) were both of them attached to Theodotus, a boy from Platæa. Theodotus was living with the plaintiff; but the defendant asserted that the boy had signed an agreement to consort with him for the consideration of three hundred drachmae, and, relying on this contract, he had attempted more than once to carry off the boy by force. Violent altercations, stone-throwings, house-breakings, and encounters of various kinds having ensued, the plaintiff brought an action for assault and battery against Simon. A modern reader is struck with the fact that he is not at all ashamed of his own relation toward Theodotus. It may be noted that the details of this action throw light upon the historic brawl at Corinth in which a boy was killed, and which led to the foundation of Syracuse by Archias the Bacchiad. ₂

Footnotes

30:4 This, by the way, is a strong argument against the theory that the *Iliad* was a post-Herodotean poem. A poet in the age of Pisistratus or Pericles would not have omitted paiderastia from his view of life, and could not have told the myth of Ganymede as Homer tells it. It is doubtful whether he could have preserved the pure outlines of the story of Patroclus.

31:1 Page 182, Jowett's trans. Mr. Jowett censures this speech as sophistic and confused in view. It is precisely on this account that it is valuable. The confusion indicates the obscure conscience of the Athenians. The sophistry is the result of a half-acknowledged false position.

32:1 Page 181. Jowett's trans.

33:1 See the curious passages in Plato, *Symp.*, p. 192; Plutarch, *Erot.*, p. 751; and Lucian, *Amores*, c. 38.

33:2 Quoted by Athen, xiii. 573 B.

34:1 As Lycon chaperoned Autolycus at the feast of Callias.--Xen. *Symp*. Boys incurred immediate suspicion if they went out alone to parties. See a fragment from the *Sappho* of Ephippus in Athen, xiii. p. 572 C.

34:2 Line 137. The joke here is that the father in Utopia suggests, of his own accord, what in Athens he carefully guarded against.

34:3 Page 222, Jowett's trans.

34:4 *Clouds*, 948 and on. I have abridged the original, doing violence to one of the most beautiful pieces of Greek poetry.

35:1 Aristophanes returns to this point below, line 1,036, where he says that Youths chatter all day in the hot baths and leave the wrestling-grounds empty.

35:2 There was a good reason for shunning each. The Agora was the meeting-place of idle gossips, the centre of chaff and scandal. The shops were, as we shall see, the resort of bad characters and panders.

35:3 Line 1,071, *et seq.*

36:1 Caps. 44, 45, 46. The quotation is only an abstract of the original.

36:2 Worn up to the age of about eighteen.

36:3 Compare with the passages just quoted two epigrams from the *Mousa Paidiké* (*Greek Anthology*, sect. 12): No. 123, from a lover to a lad who has conquered in a boxing-match; No. 192, where Straton says he prefers the dust and oil of the wrestling-ground to the curls and perfumes of a woman's robe.

37:1 Page 255 B.

37:2 1,025

37:3 *Charmides*, 153.

38:1 Lysis, 206. This seems, however, to imply that on other occasions they were separated.

38:2 Charmides, p. 154, Jowett.

38:3 Page 155, Jowett.

39:1 Cap i. 8.

39:2 See cap. viii. 7. This is said before the boy, and in his hearing.

39:3 Cap. iii. 12.

39:4 Cap. iv. 10, *et seq.* The English is an abridgment.

40:1 *Laws*, i. 636 C.

40:2 Athen., xiii. 602 D.

40:3 *Eroticus*.

40:4 Line 60, ascribed to Theocritus, but not genuine.

40:5 Athen., xiii. 609 D.

40:6 *Mousa Paidiké*, 86.

41:1 Compare the *Atys* of Catullus: "Ego mulier, ego adolescens, ego ephebus, ego puer, Ego gymnasi fui flos, ego eram decus olei."

41:2 See the law on these points in *Æsch. adv. Timarchum*.

41:3 Thus Aristophanes quoted above.

41:4 Aristoph., *Ach*., 144, and *Mousa Paidiké*, 120.

42:1 See Sir William Hamilton's *Vases*.

42:2 Lysias, according to Suidas, was the author of five Erotic epistles addressed to young men.

42:3 See Aristoph., *Plutus*, 153-159; Birds, 704-707. Cp. *Mousa Paidiké*, 44 239, 237. The boys made extraordinary demands upon their lovers generosity. The curious tale told about Alcibiades points in this direction. In Crete they did the like, but also set their lovers to execute difficult tasks as Eurystheus imposed the twelve labours on Herakles.

42:4 Page 29.

42:5 *Mousa Paidiké*, 8: cp. a fragment of Crates, *Poetæ Conic* i, Didot, p. 83.

43:1 *Comici Græci*, Didot, pp. 562, 31, 308.

43:2 It is curious to compare the passage in the second *Philippic* about the youth of Mark Antony with the story told by Plutarch about Alcibiades, who left the custody of his guardians for the house of Democrates.

43:3 See both *Lysias against Simon and Æschines against Timarchus*.

43:4 *Peace*, line 11; compare the word *Pallakion* in Plato, *Comici Græci*, p. 26 1.

43:5 Diog. Laert., ii. 105.

43:6 Plato's *Phædo*, p. 89.

44:1 *Orat. Attici*, vol. ii. p. 223.

44:2 See Herodotus. Max. Tyr. tells the story (*Dissert.*, xxiv. 1) in detail. The boy's name was Actæon, wherefore he may be compared, he says, to that other Actæon who was torn to death by his own dogs.

XIV.

We have seen in the foregoing section that paiderastia at Athens was closely associated with liberty, manly sports, severe studies, enthusiasm, self-sacrifice, self-control, and deeds of daring, by those who cared for those things. It has also been made abundantly manifest that no serious moral shame attached to persons who used boys like women, but that effeminate youths of free birth were stigmatised for their indecent profligacy. It remains still to ascertain the more delicate distinctions which were drawn by Attic law and custom in this matter, though what has been already quoted from Pausanias in the *Symposium* of Plato may be: taken fairly to express the code of honour among gentlemen.

In the *Plutus* 3 Aristophanes is careful to divide "boys with lovers," into "the good," and "the strumpets." This distinction will serve as basis for the following remarks. A very definite line was drawn by the Athenians between boys who accepted the addresses of their lovers because they liked them or because they were ambitious of comradeship with men of spirit, and those who sold their bodies for money. Minute inquiry was never instituted into the conduct of the former class; else Alcibiades could not have made his famous declaration about Socrates, 1 nor would Plato in the *Phædrus* have regarded an occasional breach of chastity, under the compulsion of violent passion, as a venial error. 2 The latter, on the other hand, besides being visited with universal censure, were disqualified by law from exercising the privileges of the franchise, from undertaking embassies, from frequenting the Agora, and from taking part in public festivals, under the penalty of death. Æschines, from whom we learn the wording of this statute, adds: 3 "This law he passed with regard to youths who sin with facility and readiness against their own bodies." He then proceeds to define the true nature of prostitution, prohibited by law to citizens of Athens. It is this: "Any one who acts in this way towards a single man, provided he do it with payment, seems to me to be liable to the reproach in question." 4 The whole discussion turns upon the word *Misthos*. The orator is cautious to meet the argument that a written contract was necessary in order to construct a case of *Hetaireia* at law. 5 In the statute, he observes, there is no mention of "contract" or "deed in writing." The offence has been sufficiently established "when in any way whatever payment has been made."

In order to illustrate the feeling of the Athenians with regard to making profit out of paiderastic relations, I may perhaps be permitted to interrupt the analysis of Æschines by referring to Xenophon's character (*Anab.* si, 6, 21) of the Strategus Menon. The whole tenor of his judgment is extremely unfavourable toward this man, who invariably pursued selfish and mean aims, debasing virtuous qualities like ambition and industry in the mere pursuit of wealth and power. He was, in fact, devoid of chivalrous feeling, good taste, and honour. About his behaviour as a youth Xenophon writes: "WithAriæus, the barbarian, because this man was partial to handsome youths, he became extremely intimate while he was still in the prime of adolescence; moreover, he had Tharypas for his beloved, he being beardless and Tharypas a man with a beard." His crime seems to have been that he prostituted himself to the barbarianAriæus in order to advance his interest, and, probably with the same view, flattered the effeminate vanity of an elder man by pretending to love him out of the right time or season. Plutarch (*Pyrrhus*) mentions this Tharypas as the first to introduce Hellenic manners among the Molossi.

When more than one lover was admitted, the guilt was aggravated. "It will then be manifest that he has not only acted the strumpet, but that he has been a common prostitute. For he who does this indifferently, and with money, and for money, seems to have incurred that designation. "Thus the question finally put to the Areopagus, in which court the case against Timarchus was tried, ran as follows, in the words of Æschines: 1 "To which of these two classes will you reckon Timarchus--to those who have had a lover, or to those who have been prostitutes?" In his rhetorical exposition Æschines defines the true character of the virtuous *Eromenos*. Frankly admitting his own partiality for beautiful young men, he argues after this fashion: 2 "I do not attach any blame to love. I do not take away the character of handsome lads. I do not deny that I have often loved, and had many quarrels and jealousies in this matter. But I establish this as an irrefutable fact, that, while the love of beautiful and temperate youths does honour to humanity and indicates a generous temper, the buying of the person of a free boy for debauchery is a mark of insolence and ill-breeding. To be loved is an honour: to sell yourself is a disgrace." He then appeals to the law which forbade slaves to love, thereby implying that this was the privilege and pride of free men. He alludes to the heroic deed of Aristogeiton and to the great example of Achilles. Finally, he draws up a list of well-known and respected citizens whose loves were notorious, and compares them with a parallel list of persons infamous for their debauchery. What remains in the peroration to this invective traverses the same ground. Some phrases may be quoted which illustrate the popular feeling of the Athenians. Timarchus is stigmatised 3 as "the man and male who in spite of this has debauched his body by womanly acts of lust," and again as "one who against the law of nature has given himself to lewdness." It is obvious here that Æschines, the self-avowed boy-lover, while seeking to crush his opponent by flinging effeminacy and unnatural behaviour in his teeth, assumes at the same time that honourable paiderastia implies no such disgrace. Again, he observes that it is as easy to recognise a pathic by his impudent behaviour as a gymnast by his muscles. Lastly, he bids the judges force intemperate lovers to abstain from free youths and satisfy their lusts upon the persons of foreigners and aliens. 1 The whole matter at this distance of time is obscure, nor can we hope to apprehend the full force of distinctions drawn by a Greek orator appealing to a Greek audience. We may, indeed, fairly presume that, as is always the case with popular ethics, considerable confusion existed in the minds of the Athenians themselves, and that even for them to formulate the whole of their social feelings on this topic consistently, would have been impossible. The main point, however, seems to be that at Athens it was held honourable to love free boys with decency; that the conduct of lovers between themselves, within the limits of recognised friendship, was not challenged; and that no particular shame attached to profligate persons so long as they refrained from tampering with the sons of citizens. ₂

Footnotes

44:3 153.

45:1 *Symph.*, 217.

45:2 *Phœdr.*, 256.

45:3 Page 17. My quotations are made from Dobson's Oratores Attici, vol. xii., and the references are to his pages.

45:4 Page 30.

45:5 Page 67.

46:1 Page 67.

46:2 Page 59.

46:3 Page 75.

47:1 Page 78.

47:2 Æschines. p. 27, apologises to Misgolas, who was a man, he says, of good breeding, for being obliged to expose his early connection with Timarchus. Misgolas, however, is more than once mentioned by the comic poets with contempt as a notorious rake.

XV.

The sources from which our information has hitherto been drawn--speeches, poems, biographies, and the dramatic parts of dialogues--yield more real knowledge about the facts of Athenian paiderastia than can be found in the speculations of philosophers. In Aristotle, for instance, paiderastia is almost conspicuous by its absence It is true that he speculates upon the Cretan customs in the *Politics*, mentions the prevalence of boy-love among the Kelts, and incidentally notices the legends of Diocles and Cleomachus; [3] but he never discusses the matter as fully as might have been expected from a philosopher whose speculations covered the whole field of Greek experience. The chapters on *Philia* in the *Ethics* might indeed have been written by a modern moralist for modern readers, though it is possible that in his treatment of "friendship with pleasure for its object" and "friendship with advantage for its object," Aristotle is aiming at the vicious sort of paiderastia. As regards his silence in the *Politics*, it is worth noticing that this treatise breaks off at the very point where we should naturally look for a scientific handling of the education of the passions, and, therefore, it is possible that we may have lost the weightiest utterance of Greek philosophy upon the matter of our enquiry.

Though Aristotle contains but little to the purpose, the case is different with Plato; nor would it be possible to omit a detailed examination of the Platonic doctrine on the topic or to neglect the attempt he made to analyse and purify a passion capable, according to his earlier philosophical speculations, of supplying the starting-point for spiritual progress.

The first point to notice in the Platonic treatment of paiderastia is the difference between the ethical opinions expressed in the *Phædrus*, *Symposium*, *Republic*, *Charmides*, and *Lysis*, on the one hand, and those expounded in the *Laws* upon the other. The *Laws*, which are probably a genuine work of Plato's old age, condemn that passion which in the *Phædrus* and *Symposium* he exalted as the greatest boon of human life and as the groundwork of the philosophical temperament; the ordinary social manifestations of which he described with sympathy in the *Lysis* and the *Charmides*, and which he viewed with more than toleration in the Republic. It is not my business to offer a solution of this contradiction; but I may observe that Socrates, who plays the part of protagonist in nearly all the other dialogues of Plato, and who, as we shall see, professed a special cult of love, is conspicuous by his absence in the *Laws*. It is, therefore, not improbable that the philosophical idealisation of paiderastia, to which the name of Platonic love is usually given, should rather be described as Socratic. However that may be, I think it will be well to deal first with the doctrine put into the mouth of the Athenian stranger in the *Laws*, and then to pass on to the consideration of what Socrates is made to say upon the subject of Greek love in the earlier dialogues.

The position assumed by Plato in the *Laws* (p. 636) is this: Syssitia and gymnasia are excellent institutions in their way, but they have a tendency to degrade natural love in man below the level of the beasts. Pleasure is only natural when it arises out of the intercourse between men and women, but the intercourse between men and men, or women and women, is contrary to nature. ₁ The bold attempt at overleaping Nature's laws was due originally to unbridled lust.

This position is developed in the eighth book (p. 836), where Plato directs his criticism, not only against what would now be termed the criminal intercourse between persons of the same sex, but also against incontinence in general. While framing a law of almost monastic rigour for the regulation of the sexual appetite, he remains an ancient Greek. He does not reach the point of view from which women are regarded as the proper objects of both passion and friendship, as the fit companions of men in all relations of life; far less does he revert to his earlier speculations upon the enthusiasm generated by a noble passion. The modern ideal of marriage and the chivalrous conception of womanhood as worthy to be worshipped are alike unknown to him. Abstinence from the delights of love, continence except for the sole end of procreation, is the rule which he proposes to the world.

There are three distinct things, Plato argues, which, owing to the inadequacy of language to represent states of thought, have been confounded. ₁ These are friendship, desire, and a third mixed species. Friendship is further described as the virtuous affection of equals in taste, age and station. Desire is always founded on a sense of contrast. While friendship is "gentle and mutual through life," desire is "fierce and wild." ₂ The true friend seeks to live chastely with the chaste object of his attachment, whose soul he loves. The lustful lover longs to enjoy the flower of his youth and cares only for the body. The third sort is mixed of these; and a lover of this composite kind is torn asunder by two impulses, "the one commanding him to enjoy the youth's person, the other forbidding him to do so." ₃ The description of the lover of the third species so exactly suits the paiderast of nobler quality in Greece, as I conceive him to have actually existed, that I shall give a full quotation of this passage: ₁--

"As to the mixed sort, which is made up of them both, there is, first of all, a difficulty in determining what he who is possessed by this third love desires; moreover, he is drawn different ways, and is in doubt between the two principles, the one exhorting him to enjoy the beauty of the youth, and the other forbidding him; for the one is a lover of the body and hungers after beauty like ripe fruit, and would fain satisfy himself without any regard to the character of the beloved; the other holds the desire of the body to be a secondary matter, and, looking rather than loving with his soul, and desiring the soul of the other in a becoming manner, regards the satisfaction of the bodily love as wantonness; be reverences and respects temperance and courage and magnanimity and wisdom, and wishes to live chastely with the chaste object of his affection."

It is remarkable that Plato, in this analysis of the three sorts of love, keeps strictly within the bounds of paiderastia. He rejects desire and the mixed sort of love, reserving friendship (*Philia*) and ordaining marriage for the satisfaction of the aphrodisiac instinct at a fitting age, but more particularly for the procreation of children. Wantonness of every description is to be made as much a sin as incest, both by law and also by the world's opinion. If Olympian victors, with an earthly crown in view, learn to live chastely for the preservation of their strength while training, shall not men whose contest is for heavenly prizes keep their bodies undefiled, their spirits holy?

Socrates, the mystagogue of amorous philosophy, is absent, as I have observed, from this discussion of the laws. I turn now to those earlier dialogues in which he expounds the doctrine of Platonic, or, as I should prefer to call it, Socratic, love. We know from Xenophon, as well as Plato, that Socrates named his philosophy the Science of Love. The one thing on which I pride myself, he says, is knowledge of all matters that pertain to love. It furthermore appears that Socrates thought himself in a peculiar sense predestined to reform and to ennoble paiderastia. "Finding this passion at its height throughout the whole of Hellas, but most especially in Athens and all places full of evil lovers and of youths seduced, he felt a pity for both parties. Not being a lawgiver like Solon, he could not stop the custom by statute nor correct it by force, nor again dissuade men from it by his eloquence. He did not, however, on that account abandon the lovers or the boys to their fate, but tried to suggest a remedy." This passage, which I have paraphrased from Maximus Tyrius, 1 sufficiently expresses the attitude assumed by Socrates in the Platonic dialogue. He sympathises with Greek lovers, and avows a fervent admiration for beauty in the persons of young men. At the same time he declares himself upon the side of temperate and generous affection, and strives to utilise the erotic enthusiasm as a motive power in the direction of philosophy. This was really nothing more or less than an attempt to educate the Athenians by appealing to their own higher instincts. We have seen that paiderastia in the prime of Hellenic culture, whatever sensual admixture it might have contained, was a masculine passion. It was closely connected with the love of political independence, with the contempt for Asiatic luxury, with the gymnastic sports, and with the intellectual interests which distinguished Hellenes from barbarians. Partly owing to the social habits of their cities, and partly to the peculiar notions which they entertained regarding the seclusion of free women in the home, all the higher elements of spiritual and mental activity, and the conditions under which a generous passion was conceivable, had become the exclusive privileges of men. It was not that women occupied a semi-servile station, as some students have imagined, or that within the sphere of the household they were not the respected and trusted helpmates of men. But circumstances rendered it impossible for them to excite romantic and enthusiastic passion. The exaltation of the emotions was reserved for the male sex.

Socrates, therefore, sought to direct and moralise a force already existing. In the *Phœdrus* he describes the passion of love between man and boy as a madness, not different in quality from that which inspires poets; and, after painting that fervid picture of the lover, he declares that the true object of a noble life can only be attained by passionate friends, bound together in the chains of close yet temperate comradeship, seeking always to advance in knowledge, self-restraint, and intellectual illumination. The doctrine of the *Symposium* is not different, except that Socrates here takes a higher flight. The same love is treated as the method whereby the soul may begin her mystic journey to the region of essential beauty, truth, and goodness. It has frequently been remarked that Plato's dialogues have to be read as poems even more than as philosophical treatises; and if this be true at all, it is particularly true of both the *Phædrus* and the *Symposium*. The lesson which both essays seem intended to inculcate is this: love, like poetry and prophecy, is a divine gift, which diverts men from the common current of their lives; but in the right use of this gift lies the secret of all human excellence. The passion which grovels in the filth of sensual grossness may be transformed into a glorious enthusiasm, a winged splendour, capable of soaring to the contemplation of eternal verities. How strange will it be, when once those heights of intellectual intuition have been scaled, to look down again to earth and view the *Meirakidia* in whom the soul first recognised the form of beauty! 1 There is a deeply rooted mysticism, an impenetrable soofyism, in the Socratic doctrine of Erôs.

In the *Phædrus*, the *Symposium*, the *Charmides*, the *Lysis*, and the *Republic*, Plato dramatised the real Socrates, while he gave liberal scope to his own personal sympathy for paiderastia. 2 In the *Laws*, if we accept this treatise as the work of his old age, he discarded the Socratic mask, and wrote a kind of palinode, which indicates more moral growth than pure disapprobation of the paiderastic passion. I have already tried to show that the point of view in the *Laws* is still Greek: that their author has not passed beyond the sphere of Hellenic ethics. He has only become more ascetic in his rule of conduct as the years advanced, importing the *rumores senum severiorum* into his discourse, and recognising the imperfection of that halting-point between the two logical extremes of Pagan license and monastic asceticism which in the fervour of his greener age he advocated. As a young man, Plato felt sympathy for love so long as it was paiderastic and not spent on women; he even condoned a lapse through warmth of feeling into self-indulgence. As an old man, he denounced carnal pleasure of all kinds, and sought to limit the amative instincts to the one sole end of procreation.

It has so happened that Plato's name is still connected with the ideal of passion purged from sensuality. Much might be written about the parallel between the *mania* of the *Phædrus* and the *joy* of medieval amorists. Nor would it be unprofitable to trace the points of contact between the love described by Dante in the *Vita Nuova* and the paiderastia exalted to the heavens by Plato. 1 The spiritual passion for Beatrice which raised the Florentine poet above vile things, and led him by the philosophic paths of the *Convito* to the beatific vision of the *Paradiso*, bears no slight resemblance to the *Erôs* of the *Symposium*. Yet we know that Dante could not have studied Plato's works; and the specific love which Plato praised he sternly stigmatised. The harmony between Greek and mediæval mysticism in this matter of the emotions rests on something permanent in human nature, common alike to paiderastia and to chivalrous enthusiasm for woman.

It would be well worth raising here the question whether there was not something special both in the Greek consciousness itself and also in the conditions under which it reached maturity, which justified the Socratic attempt to idealise paiderastia. Placed upon the borderland of barbarism, divided from the Asiatic races by an acute but narrow line of demarcation, the Greeks had arrived at the first free notion of the spirit in its disentanglement from matter and from symbolism. But this notion of the spirit was still æsthetic, rather than strictly ethical or rigorously scientific. In the Greek gods intelligence is perfected and character is well defined; but these gods are always concrete persons, with corporeal forms adapted to their spiritual essence. The interpenetration of spiritual and corporeal elements in a complete personality, the transfusion of intellectual and emotional faculties throughout a physical organism exactly suited to their adequate expression, marks Greek religion and Greek art. What the Greeks worshipped in their ritual, what they represented in their sculpture, was always personality--the spirit and the flesh in amity and mutual correspondence; the spirit burning through the flesh and moulding it to individual forms; the flesh providing a fit dwelling for the spirit which controlled and fashioned it. Only philosophers among the Greeks attempted to abstract the spirit as a self-sufficient, independent, conscious entity; and these philosophers were few, and what they wrote or spoke had little direct influence upon the people. This being the mental attitude of the Greek race, it followed as a necessity that their highest emotional aspirations, their purest personal service, should be devoted to clear and radiant incarnations of the spirit in a living person. They had never been taught to regard the body with a sense of shame, but rather to admire it as the temple of the spirit, and to accept its needs and instincts with natural acquiescence. Male beauty disengaged for them the passion it inspired from service of domestic, social, civic duties. The female form aroused desire, but it also suggested maternity and obligations of the household. The male form was the most perfect image of the deity, self-contained, subject to no necessities of impregnation, determined in its action only by the laws of its own reason and its own volition.

Quite a different order of ideas governed the ideal adopted by mediæval chivalry, The spirit in its self-sufficingness, detached from the body, antagonistic to the body, had been divinised by Christianity. Woman regarded as a virgin and at the same time a mother, the maiden-mother of God made man, had been exalted to the throne of heaven. The worship of woman became, by a natural and logical process, the correlative in actual human life for that worship of the incarnate Deity which was the essence of religion. A remarkable point in mediæval love is that the sensual appetites were, theoretically at least, excluded from the homage paid to woman. It was not the wife or the mistress, but the lady, who inspired the knight. Dante had children by Gemma, Petrarch had children by an unknown concubine, but it was the sainted Beatrice, it was the unattainable Laura, who received the homage of Dante and of Petrarch.

In like manner the sensual appetites were, theoretically at least, excluded from Platonic paiderastia. It was the divine in human flesh--"the radiant sight of the beloved," to quote from Plato; "the fairest and most intellectual of earthly bodies," to borrow a phrase from Maximus Tyrius--it was this which stimulated the Greek lover, just as a similar incarnation of divinity inspired the chivalrous lover, Thus we might argue that the Platonic conception of paiderastia furnishes a close analogue to the chivalrous devotion to women, due regard being paid to the differences which existed between the plastic ideal of Greek religion and the romantic ideal of mediæval Christianity. The one veiled adultery, the other sodomy. That in both cases the conception was rarely realised in actual life only completes the parallel.

To pursue this inquiry further is, however, alien to my task. It is enough to have indicated the psychological agreement in respect of purified affection which underlay two such apparently antagonistic ideals of passion. Few modern writers, when they speak with admiration or contempt of Platonic love, reflect that in its origin this phrase denoted an absorbing passion for young men. The Platonist, as appears from numerous passages in the Platonic writings, would have despised the Petrarchist as a vulgar woman-lover The Petrarchist would have loathed the Platonist as a moral Pariah. Yet Platonic love, in both its Attic and its mediæval manifestations, was one and the same thing.

The philosophical ideal of paiderastia in Greece which bore the names of Socrates and Plato met with little but contempt. Cicero, in a passage which has been echoed by Gibbon, remarked upon "the thin device of virtue and friendship which amused the philosophers of Athens." [1] Epicurus criticised the Stoic doctrine of paiderastia by sententiously observing that philosophers only differed from the common race of men in so far as they could better cloak their vice with sophistries. This severe remark seems justified by the opinions ascribed to Zeno by Plutarch, Sextus Empiricus, and Stobæus. [2] But it may be doubted whether the real drift of the Stoic theory of love, founded on *Adiaphopha*, was understood. Lucian, in the *Amores*, [3] makes Charicles, the advocate of love for women, deride the Socratic ideal as vain nonsense, while Theomnestus, the man of pleasure, to whom the dispute is finally referred, decides that the philosophers are either fools or humbugs. [4] Daphnæus, in the erotic dialogue of Plutarch, arrives at a similar conclusion; and, in an essay on education, the same author contends that no prudent father would allow the sages to enter into intimacy with his sons. ₅ The discredit incurred by philosophers in the later age of Greek culture is confirmed by more than one passage in Petronius and Juvenal, while Athenæus especially inveighs against philosophic lovers as acting against nature. ₆ The attempt of the Platonic Socrates to elevate without altering the morals of his race may therefore be said fairly to have failed. Like his republic, his love existed only in heaven.

Footnotes

47:3 See *Pol.*, ii. 7, 5; ii. 6, 5; ii. 9, 6.

48:1 The advocates of paiderastia in Greece tried to refute the argument from animals (*Laws*, p. 636 B: cp. *Daphnis and Chloe*, lib. 4, what Daphnis says to Gnathon) by, the following considerations: Man is not a lion or a bear. Social life among human beings is highly artificial; forms of intimacy unknown to the natural state are therefore to be regarded, like clothing, cooking of food, houses, machinery, &c., as the invention and privilege of rational beings. See Lucian, *Amores*, 33, 34, 35, 36, for a full exposition of this argument. See also *Mousa Paidiké*, 245. The curious thing is that many animals are addicted to all sorts of so-called unnatural vices.

49:1 Maximus Tyrius, who, in the rhetorical analysis of love alluded to before (p. 172), has closely followed Plato, insists upon the confusion introduced by language, *Dissert.*, xxiv. 3. Again, *Dissert.*, xxvi. 4; and compare *Dissert.*, xxv. 4.

49:2 This is the development of the argument in the Phædrus, where Socrates, improvising an improvement on the speech of Lysias, compares lovers to wolves and boys to lambs. See the passage in Max. Tyr., where Socrates is compared to a shepherd, the Athenian lovers to butchers, and the boys to lambs upon the mountains.

49:3 This again is the development of the whole eloquent analysis of love, as it attacks the uninitiated and unphilosophic nature, in the *Phædrus*.

50:1 Jowett's trans., p. 837.

51:1 *Dissert.*, xxv. r. The same author pertinently remarks that, though the teaching of Socrates on love might well have been considered perilous, it formed no part of the accusations of either Anvtus or Aristophanes. *Dissert.*, xxiv. 5-7.

52:1 This is a remark of Diotima's. Maximus Tyrius (*Dissert.*, xxvi. 8) gives it a very rational interpretation. Nowhere else, he says, but in the human form, does the light of the divine beauty shine so clear. This is the word of classic art, the word of the humanities, to use a phrase of the Renaissance. it finds an echo in many beautiful sonnets of Michelangelo.

52:2 See Bergk., vol. ii. pp. 616-629, for a critique of the canon of the highly paiderastic epigrams which bear Plato's name and for their text.

53:1 I select the *Vita Nuova* as the most eminent example of mediaeval erotic mysticism.

XVI.

Philip of Macedon, when he pronounced the panegyric of the Sacred Band at Chæronea, uttered the funeral oration of Greek love in its nobler forms. With the decay of military spirit and the loss of freedom, there was no sphere left for that type of comradeship which I attempted to describe in Section IV. The philosophical ideal, to which some cultivated Attic thinkers had aspired, remained unrealised, except, we may perhaps suppose, in isolated instances. Meanwhile paiderastia as a vice did not diminish. It only grew more wanton and voluptuous. Little, therefore, can be gained by tracing its historical development further, although it is not without interest to note the mode of feeling and the opinion of some later poets and rhetoricians.

The idyllists are the only poets, if we except a few epigrammatists of the *Anthology*, who preserve a portion of the old heroic sentiment. No true student of Greek literature will have felt that he could strictly censure the paiderastic passages of the *Thalysia, Aïtes, Hylas, Paidika*. They have the ring of genuine and respectable emotion. This may also be said about the two fragments of Bion which begin *Hespere tas eratas* and *Olbioi oi phileontes*. The *Duserôs*, ascribed without due warrant to Theocritus, is in many respects a beautiful composition, but it lacks the fresh and manly touches of the master's style, and bears the stamp of an unwholesome rhetoric. Why, indeed, should we pity this suicide, and why should the statue of Love have fallen on the object of his admiration? Maximus Tyrius showed more sense when he contemptuously wrote about those men who killed themselves for love of a beautiful lad in Locri: [1] "And in good sooth they deserved to die."

The dialogue entitled *Erotes*, attributed to Lucian, deserves a paragraph. More than any other composition of the rhetorical age of Greek literature, it attempts a comprehensive treatment of erotic passion, and sums up the teaching of the doctors and the predilections of the vulgar in one treatise. [2] Like many of Lucian's compositions, it has what may be termed a retrospective and resumptive value. That is to say, it represents less the actual feeling of the author and his age than the result of his reading and reflection brought into harmony with his experience. The scene is laid at Cnidus in the groves of Aphrodite. The temple and the garden and the statue of Praxiteles are described with a luxury of language which strikes the keynote of the dialogue. We have exchanged the company of Plato, Xenophon, or Æschines for that of a Juvenalian *Græculus*, a delicate æsthetic voluptuary. Every epithet smells of musk and every phrase is a provocative. The interlocutors are Callicratides the Athenian and Charicles the Rhodian. Callicratides kept an establishment of *exoleti*; when the down upon their chins had grown beyond the proper point--"when the beard is just sprouting, when youth is in the prime of charm," they were drafted off to farms and country villages. Charicles maintained a harem of dancing-girls and flute-players. The one was "madly passionate for lads;" the other no less "mad for women."

Charicles undertook the cause of women, Callicratides that of boys. Charicles began, The love of women is sanctioned by antiquity; it is natural; it endures through life; it alone provides pleasure for both sexes. Boys grow bearded, rough, and past their prime. Women always excite passion. Then Callicratides takes up his parable. Masculine love combines virtue with pleasure. While the love of women is a physical necessity, the love of boys is a product of high culture and an adjunct of philosophy. Paiderastia may be either vulgar or celestial; the second will be sought by men of liberal education and good manners. Then follow contrasted pictures of the lazy woman and the manly youth. The one provokes to sensuality, the other excites noble emulation in the ways of virile living. Lucian, summing up the arguments of the two pleaders, decides that Corinth must give way to Athens, adding, "Marriage is open to all men, but the love of boys to philosophers only." This verdict is referred to Theomnestus, a Don Juan of both sexes. He replies that both boys and women are good for pleasure; the philosophical arguments of Callicratides are cant.

This brief abstract of Lucian's dialogue on love indicates the cynicism with which its author viewed the subject, using the whole literature and all the experience of the Greeks to support a thesis of pure hedonism. The sybarites of Cairo or Constantinople at the present moment might employ the same arguments, except that they would omit the philosophic cant of Callicratides.

There is nothing in extant Greek literature of a date anterior to the Christian era which is foul in the same sense as that in which the works of Roman poets (Catullus and Martial), Italian poets (Beccatelli and Baffo), and French poets (Scarron and Voltaire) are foul. Only purblind students will be unable to perceive the difference between the obscenity of the Latin races and that of Aristophanes. The difference, indeed, is wide and radical, and strongly marked.

It is the difference between a race naturally gifted with a delicate, aesthetic sense of beauty, and one in whom that sense was always subject to the perturbation of gross instincts. But with the first century of the new age a change came over even the imagination of the Greeks. Though they never lost their distinction of style, that precious gift of lightness and good taste conferred upon them with thew language, they borrowed something of their conquerors' vein, This makes itself felt in the *Anthology*. Straton and Rufinus suffered the contamination of the Roman genius, stronger in political organisation than that of Hellas, but coarser and less spiritually tempered in morals and in art. Straton was a native of Sardis who flourished in the second century. He compiled a book of paiderastic poems, consisting in a great measure of his own and Meleager's compositions, which now forms the twelfth section of the *Palatine Anthology*. This book he dedicated, not to the Muse, but to Zeus; for Zeus was the boy-lover among deities; [1] he bade it carry forth his message to fair youths throughout the world; [2] and he claimed a special inspiration from heaven for singing of one sole subject, paiderastia. ₃ It may be said with truth that Straton understood the bent of his own genius. We trace a blunt earnestness of intention in his epigrams, a certainty of feeling and directness of artistic treatment, which show that he had only one object in view. Meleager has far higher qualities as a poet, and his feeling. as well as his style, is more exquisite. But he wavered between the love of boys and women, seeking in both the satisfaction of emotional yearnings which in the modern world would have marked him as a sentimentalist. The so-called *Mousa Paidiké*, "Muse of Boyhood," is a collection of two hundred and fifty-eight short poems, some of them of great artistic merit, in praise of boys and boy-love. The common-places of these epigrams are Ganymede and Erôs; ₄ we hear but little of Aphrodite-her domain is the other section of the *Anthology*, called Erotika. A very small percentage of these compositions can be described as obscene; ₅ none are nasty in the style of Martial or Ausonius; some are exceedingly picturesque; ₆ a few are written in a strain of lofty or of lovely music; ₇ one or two are delicate and subtle in their humour. ₈ The whole collection supplies good means of judging how the Greeks of the decadence felt about this form of love. *Malakia* is the real condemnation of this poetry, rather than brutality or coarseness. A favourite topic is the superiority of boys over girls. This sometimes takes a gross form; ₁ but once or twice the treatment of the subject touches a real psychological distinction, as in the following epigram: ₂--

"The love of women is not after my heart's desire; but the fires of male desire have placed me under inextinguishable coals of burning. The heat there is mightier; for the more powerful is male than female, the keener is that desire."

These four lines give the key to much of the Greek preference for paiderastia. The love of the male, when it has been apprehended and entertained, is more exciting, they thought, more absorbent of the whole nature, than the love of the female. It is, to use another kind of phraseology, more of a mania and more of a disease.

With the *Anthology* we might compare the curious *Epistolai Erotikai* of Philostratus. ₃ They were in all probability rhetorical compositions, not intended for particular persons; yet they indicate the kind of wooing to which youths were subjected in later Hellas. ₄ The discrepancy between the triviality of their subject-matter and the exquisiteness of their diction is striking. The second of these qualities has made them a mine for poets. Ben Jonson, for example, borrowed the loveliest of his lyrics from the following *concetto*:--"I sent thee a crown of roses, not so much honouring thee, though this, too, was my meaning, but wishing to do some kindness to the roses that they might not wither." Take, again, the phrase, "Well, and love himself is naked, and the graces and the stars;" or this, "O rose, that has a voice to speak with!"--or this metaphor for the footsteps of the beloved, "O rhythms of most beloved feet, O kisses pressed upon the ground!"

While the paiderastia of the Greeks was sinking into grossness, effeminacy, and aesthetic prettiness, the moral instincts of humanity began to assert themselves in earnest. It became part of the higher doctrine of the Roman Stoics to suppress this form of passion. ₅ The Christians, from St. Paul onwards, instituted an uncompromising crusade against it. Theirs was no mere speculative warfare, like that of the philosophers at Athens. They fought with all the forces of their manhood, with the sword of the Lord and with the excommunications of the Church, to suppress what seemed to them an unutterable scandal. Dio Chrysostom, Clemens Alexandrinus, and Athanasius, are our best authorities for the vices which prevailed in Hellas during the Empire; ₁ the Roman law, moreover, proves that the civil governors aided the Church in its attempt to moralise the people on this point.

Footnotes

55:1 Tusc., iv. 33; Decline and Fall, cap. xliv. note 192.

55:2 See Meier, cap. 15.

55:3 Cap. 23.

55:4 Cap. 54.

55:5 Page 4.

55:6 It is noticeable that in all ages men of learning have been obnoxious to paiderastic passions. Dante says (Inferno, xv. 106):--

> "In somma sappi, che tutti fur cherci,
> E letterati grandi e di gran fama,
> D' un medesmo peccato al mondo lerci."

Compare Ariosto, *Satire*, vii.

56:1 *Dissert.*, xxvi. 9.

56:2 I am aware that the genuineness of the essay has been questioned.

58:1 *Mousa Paidiké*, i.

58:2 *Ibid.*, 208.

58:3 *Ibid.*, 258, 2.

58:4 *Ibid.*, 70, 65, 69, 194, 220, 221, 67, 68, 78, and others.

58:5 Perhaps ten are of this sort.

58:6 8, 125, for example.

58:7 132, 256, 221.

58:8 219.

59:1 7.

59:2 17. Compare 86.

59:3 Ed. Kayser, pp. 343-366.

59:4 It is worth comparing the letters of Philostratus with those of Alciphron, a contemporary of Lucian. In the latter there is no hint of paiderastia. The life of parasites, grisettes, lorettes, and young men about town at Athens is set forth in imitation probably of the later comedy Athens is shown to have been a Paris *à la Murger*.

59:5 See the introduction by Marcus Aurelius to his *Meditations*.

XVII.

The transmutation of Hellas proper into part of the Roman Empire, and the intrusion of Stoicism and Christianity into the sphere of Hellenic thought and feeling, mark the end of the Greek age. It still remains, however, to consider the relation of this passion to the character of the race, and to determine its influence.

In the fifth section of this essay I asserted that it is now impossible to ascertain whether the Greeks derived paiderastia from any of the surrounding nations, and if so, from which. Homer's silence makes it probable that the contact of Hellenic with Phoenician traders in the post-heroic period led to the adoption by the Greek race of a custom which they speedily assimilated and stamped with an Hellenic character. At the same time I suggested in the tenth section that paiderastia, in its more enthusiastic and martial form, may have been developed within the very sanctuary of Greek national existence by the Dorians, matured in the course of their migrations, and systematised after their settlement in Crete and Sparta. That the Greeks themselves regarded Crete as the classic ground of paiderastia favours either theory, and suggests a fusion of them both; for the geographical position of this island made it the meeting-place of Hellenes with the Asiatic races, while it was also one of the earliest Dorian acquisitions.

When we come to ask why this passion struck roots so deep into the very heart and brain of the Greek nation, we must reject the favourite hypothesis of climate. Climate is, no doubt, powerful to a great extent in determining the complexion of sexual morality; yet, as regards paiderastia we have abundant proof that nations of the North and of the South have, according to circumstances quite independent of climatic conditions, been both equally addicted and equally averse to this habit. The Etruscan, the Chinese, the ancient Keltic tribes, the Tartar hordes of Timour Khan, the Persians under Moslem rule--races sunk in the sloth of populous cities as well as the nomadic children of the Asian steppes, have all acquired a notoriety at least equal to that of the Greeks. The only difference between these people and the Greeks in respect to paiderastia is that everything which the Greek genius touched acquired a portion of its distinction, so that what in semi-barbarous society may be ignored as vice, in Greece demands attention as a phase of the spiritual life of a world-historic nation.

Like climate, ethnology must also be eliminated. It is only a superficial philosophy of history which is satisfied with the nomenclature of Semitic, Aryan, and so forth; which imagines that something is gained for, the explanation of a complex psychological problem when hereditary affinities have been demonstrated. The deeps of national personality are far more abysmal than this. Granting that climate and descent are elements of great importance, the religious and moral principles, the æsthetic apprehensions, and the customs which determine the character of a race leave always something still to be analysed. In dealing with Greek paiderastia, we are far more likely to reach a probable solution if we confine our attention to the specific social conditions which fostered the growth of this passion in Greece, and to the general habit of mind which permitted its evolution out of the common stuff of humanity, than if we dilate at ease upon the climate of the Ægean, or discuss the ethnical complexion of the Hellenic stock. In others words, it was the Pagan view of human life and duty which gave scope to paiderastia, while certain special Greek customs aided its development.

The Greeks themselves, quoted more than once above, have put us on the right track in this inquiry. However paiderastia began in Hellas, it was encouraged by gymnastics and syssitia. Youths and boys engaged together in athletic exercises, training their bodies to the highest point of physical attainment, growing critical about the points and proportions of the human form, lived of necessity in an atmosphere of mutual attention. Young men could not be insensible to the grace of boys in whom the bloom of beauty was unfolding. Boys could not fail to admire the strength and goodliness of men displayed in the comeliness of perfected development. Having exercised together in the wrestling-ground, the same young men and boys consorted at the common tables. Their talk fell naturally upon feats of strength and training; nor was it unnatural, in the absence of a powerful religious prohibition, that love should spring from such discourse and intercourse.

The nakedness which Greek custom permitted in gymnastic games and some religious rites no doubt contributed to the erotic force of masculine passion; and the history of their feeling upon this point deserves notice. Plato, in the *Republic* (452), observes that "not long ago the Greeks were of the opinion, which is still generally received among the barbarians, that the sight of a naked man was ridiculous and unseemly." He goes on to mention the Cretans and the Lacedæmonians as the institutors of naked games. To these conditions may he added dances in public, the ritual of gods like Erôs, ceremonial processions, and contests for the prize of beauty.

The famous passage in the first book of Thucydides (cap. vi.) illustrates the same point. While describing the primitive culture of the Hellenes he thinks it worth while to mention that the Spartans, who first stripped themselves for running and wrestling, abandoned the girdle which it was usual to wear around the loins. He sees in this habit one of the strongest points of distinction between the Greeks and barbarians. Herodotus insists upon the same point (book i. 10), which is further confirmed by the verse of Ennius: Flagitii, &c.

The nakedness which Homer (Iliad, xxii. 66) and Tyrtæus (i. 21) describes as shameful and unseemly is that of an old man. Both poets seem to imply that a young man's naked body is beautiful even in death.

We have already seen that paiderastia as it existed in early Hellas was a martial institution, and that it never wholly lost its virile character. This suggests the consideration of another class of circumstances which were in the highest degree conducive to its free development. The Dorians, to begin with, lived like regiments of soldiers in barracks. The duty of training the younger men was thrown upon the elder; so that the close relations thus established in a race which did not positively discountenance the love of male for male rather tended actively to encourage it. Nor is it difficult to understand why the romantic emotions in such a society were more naturally aroused by male companions than by women. Matrimony was not a matter of elective affinity between two persons seeking to spend their lives agreeably and profitably in common, so much as an institution used by the state for raising vigorous recruits for the national army. All that is known about the Spartan marriage customs, taken together with Plato's speculations about a community of wives, proves this conclusively. It followed that the relation of the sexes to each other was both more formal and more simple than it is with us; the natural and the political purposes of cohabitation were less veiled by those personal and emotional considerations which play so large a part in modern life. There was less scope for the emergence of passionate enthusiasm between men and women, while the full conditions of a spiritual attachment, solely determined by reciprocal inclination, were only to be found in comradeship. In the wrestling-ground, at the common tables, in the ceremonies of religion, at the Pan-hellenic games, in the camp, in the hunting-field, on the benches of the council chamber, and beneath the porches of the Agora, men were all in all unto each other. Women meanwhile kept the house at home, gave birth to babies, and reared children till such time as the state thought fit to undertake their training. It is, moreover, well known that the age at which boys were separated from their mothers was tender. Thenceforth they lived with persons of their own sex; their expanding feelings were confined within the sphere of masculine experience until the age arrived when marriage had to be considered in the light of a duty to the commonwealth. How far this tended to influence the growth of sentiment and to determine its quality may be imagined.

In the foregoing paragraph I have restricted my attention almost wholly to the Dorians: but what has just been said about the circumstance of their social life suggests a further consideration regarding paiderastia at large among the Greeks, which takes rank with the weightiest of all. The peculiar status of Greek women is a subject surrounded with difficulty; yet no one can help feeling that the idealisation of masculine love, which formed so prominent a feature of Greek life in the historic period, was intimately connected with the failure of the race to give their proper sphere in society to women. The Greeks themselves were not directly conscious of this fact; nor can I remember any passage in which a Greek has suggested that boy-love, flourished precisely upon the special ground which had been wrested from the right domain of the other sex. Far in advance of the barbarian tribes around them, they could not well discern the defects of their own civilisation; nor was it to be expected that they should have anticipated that exaltation of the love of women into a semi-religious cult which was the later product of chivalrous Christianity. We from the standpoint of a more fully organised society, detect their errors and pronounce that paiderastia was a necessary consequence of their unequal social culture; nor do we fail to notice that just as paiderastia was a post-Homeric intrusion into Greek life, so women, after the age of the Homeric poems, suffered a corresponding depression in the social scale. In the *Iliad* and the *Odyssey*, and in the tragedies which deal with the heroic age, they play a part of importance for which the actual conditions of historic Hellas offered no opportunities.

It was at Athens that the social disadvantages of women told with greatest force; and this perhaps may help to explain the philosophic idealisation of boy-love among the Athenians. To talk familiarly with free women on the deepest subjects, to treat them as intellectual companions, or to choose them as associates in undertakings of political moment, seems never to have entered the mind of an Athenian. Women were conspicuous by their absence from all places of resort--from the palæstra, the theatre, the Agora, Pnyx, the law-court, the symposium; and it was here, and here alone, that the spiritual energies of the men expanded. Therefore, as the military ardour of the Dorians naturally associated itself with paiderastia, so the characteristic passion of the Athenians for culture took the same direction. The result in each case was a highly wrought psychical condition, which, however alien to our instincts, must be regarded as an exaltation of the race above its common human needs--as a manifestation of fervid, highly pitched emotional enthusiasm.

It does not follow from the facts which I have just discussed that, either at Athens or at Sparta, women were excluded from an important position in the home, or that the family in Greece was not the sphere of female influence more active than the extant fragments of Greek literature reveal to us. The women of Sophocles and Euripides, and the noble ladies described by Plutarch, warn us to be cautious in our conclusions on this topic. The fact, however, remains that in Greece, as in mediæval Europe, the home was not regarded as the proper sphere for enthusiastic passion: both paiderastia and chivalry ignored the family, while the latter even set the matrimonial tie at nought. It is therefore precisely at this point of the family, regarded as a comparatively undeveloped factor in the higher spiritual life of Greeks, that the two problems of paiderastia and the position of women in Greece intersect.

In reviewing the external circumstances which favoured paiderastia, it may be added, as a minor cause, that the leisure in which the Greeks lived, supported by a crowd of slaves, and attending chiefly to their physical and mental culture, rendered them peculiarly liable to pre-occupations of passion and pleasure-seeking. In the early periods, when war was incessant, this abundance of spare time, bore less corrupt fruit than during the stagnation into which the Greeks enslaved by Macedonia and Rome declined.

So far, I have been occupied in the present section with the specific conditions of Greek society which may be regarded as determining the growth of paiderastia. With respect to the general habit of mind which caused the Greeks, in contradistinction to the Jews and Christians, to tolerate this form of feeling, it will be enough here to remark that Paganism could have nothing logically to say against it. The further consideration of this matter I shall reserve for the next division of my essay, contenting myself for the moment with the observation that Greek religion and the instincts of the Greek race offered no direct obstacle to the expansion of a habit which was strongly encouraged by the circumstances I have just enumerated.

Footnotes

60:1 See quotations in Rosenbaum, 119-140.

61:1 See Athen., xii. 5 17, for an account of their grotesque sensuality.

XVIII.

Upon a topic of great difficulty, which is, however, inseparable from the subject-matter of this inquiry, I shall not attempt to do more than to offer a few suggestions. This is the relation of paiderastia to Greek art. Whoever may have made a study of antique sculpture will not have failed to recognise its healthy human tone, its ethical rightness. There is no partiality for the beauty of the male sex, no endeavour to reserve for the masculine deities the nobler attributes of man's intellectual and moral nature, no extravagant attempt to refine upon masculine qualities by the blending of feminine voluptuousness. Aphrodite and Artemis hold their place beside Erôs and Hermes. Ares is less distinguished by the genius lavished on him than Athene. Hera takes rank with Zeus, the Nymphs with the Fauns, the Muses with Apollo. Nor are even the minor statues, which belong to decorative rather than high art, noticeable for the attribution of sensual beauties to the form of boys. This, which is certainly true of the best age, is, with rare exceptions, true of all the ages of Greek plastic art. No prurient effeminacy degraded, deformed, or unduly confounded the types of sex idealised in sculpture.

The first reflection which must occur to even prejudiced observers is that paiderastia did not corrupt the Greek imagination to any serious extent. The license of Paganism found appropriate expression in female forms, but hardly touched the male; nor would it, I think, be possible to demonstrate that obscene works of painting or of sculpture were provided for paiderastic sensualists similar to those pornographic object's which fill the reserved cabinet of the Neapolitan Museum. Thus, the testimony of Greek art might be used to confirm the asseveration of Greek literature, that among free men, at least, and gentle, this passion tended even to purify feelings which in their lust for women verged on profligacy. For one androgynous statue of Hermaphroditus or Dionysus there are at least a score of luxurious Aphrodites and voluptuous Bacchantes. Erôs; himself, unless he is portrayed, according to the Roman type of Cupid, as a mischievous urchin, is a youth whose modesty is no less noticeable than his beauty. His features are not unfrequently shadowed with melancholy, as appears in the so-called Genius of the Vatican, and in many statues which might pass for genii of silence or of sleep as well as love. It would be difficult to adduce a single wanton Erôs, a single image of this god provocative of sensual desires. There is not one before which we could say--The sculptor of that statue had sold his soul to paiderastic lust. Yet Erôs it may be remembered, was the special patron of paiderastia.

Greek art, like Greek mythology, embodied a finely graduated half-unconscious analysis of human nature. The mystery of procreation was indicated by phalli on the Hermæ. Unbridled appetite found incarnation in Priapus, who, moreover, was never a Greek god, but a Lampsacene adopted from the Asian coast by the Romans. The natural desires were symbolised in Aphrodite Praxis, Kallipugos, or Pandemos. The higher sexual enthusiasm assumed celestial form in Aphrodite Ouranios. Love itself appeared personified in the graceful Erôs of Praxiteles; and how sublimely Pheidias presented this god to the eyes of his worshippers can now only be guessed at from a mutilated fragment among the Elgin marbles. The wild and native instincts, wandering, untutored and untamed, which still connect man with the life of woods and beasts and April hours, received half-human shape in Pan and Silenus, the Satyrs and the Fauns. In this department of semi-bestial instincts we find one solitary instance bearing upon paiderastia. The group of a Satyr tempting a youth at Naples stands alone among numerous similar compositions which have female or hermaphroditic figures, and which symbolise the violent and comprehensive lust of brutal appetite. Further distinctions between the several degrees of love were drawn by the Greek artists. Himeros, the desire that strikes the spirit through the eyes, and Pothos, the longing of souls in separation from the object of their passion, were carved together with Erôs by Scopas for Aphrodite's temple at Megara. Throughout the whole of this series there is no form set aside for paiderastia, as might have been expected if the fancy of the Greeks had idealised a sensual Asiatic passion. Statues of Ganymede carried to heaven by the eagle are, indeed, common enough in Græco-Roman plastic art; yet even here there is nothing which indicates the preference for a specifically voluptuous type of male beauty.

It should be noticed that the mythology of the Greeks was determined before paiderastia laid hold upon the race. Homer and Hesiod, says Herodotus, made the Hellenic theogony, and Homer and Hesiod knew only of the passions and emotions which are common to all healthy semi-civilised humanity. The artists, therefore, found in myths and poems subject-matter which imperatively demanded a no less careful study of the female than of the male form; nor were beautiful women wanting. Great cities placed their maidens at the disposition of sculptors and painters for the modelling of Aphrodite. The girls of Sparta in their dances suggested groups of Artemis and Oreads. The Hetairai of Corinth presented every detail of feminine perfection freely to the gaze. Eyes accustomed to the "dazzling vision" of a naked athlete were no less sensitive to the virginal veiled grace of the Athenian Canephoroi. The temples of the female deities had their staffs of priestesses, and the oracles their inspired prophetesses. Remembering these facts, remembering also what we read about Æolian ladies who gained fame by poetry, there is every reason to understand how sculptors found it easy to idealise the female form. Nor need we imagine, because Greek literature abounds in references to paiderastia, and because this passion played an important part in Greek history, that therefore the majority of the race were not susceptible in a far higher degree to female charms. On the contrary, our best authorities speak of boy-love as a characteristic which distinguished warriors, gymnasts, poets, and philosophers from, the common multitude. As far as regards artists, the anecdotes which are preserved about them turn chiefly upon their preference for women. For one tale concerning the Pantarkes of Pheidias, we have a score relating to the Campaspe of Apelles and the Phryne of Praxiteles.

It may be judged superfluous to have proved that the female form was idealised in sculpture by the Hellenes at least as nobly as the male; nor need we seek elaborate reasons why paiderastia left no perceptible stain upon the art of a race distinguished before all things by the reserve of good taste. At the same time, there can be no reasonable doubt that the artistic temperament of the Greeks had something to do with its wide diffusion and many-sided development. Sensitive to every form of loveliness, and unrestrained by moral or religious prohibition, they could not fail to be enthusiastic for that corporeal beauty, unlike all other beauties of the human form, which marks male adolescence no less triumphantly than does the male soprano voice upon the point of breaking. The power of this corporeal loveliness to sway their imagination by its unique æsthetic charm is abundantly illustrated in the passages which I have quoted above from the *Charmides* of Plato and Xenophon's *Symposium*. An expressive Greek phrase, "youths in their prime of adolescence, but not distinguished by a special beauty," recognises the persuasive influence, separate from that of true beauty, which belongs to a certain period of masculine growth. The very evanescence of this "bloom of youth" made it in Greek eyes desirable, since nothing more clearly characterises the poetic myths which adumbrate their special sensibility than the pathos of a blossom 'that must fade. When distinction of feature and symmetry of form were added to this charm of youthfulness, the Greeks admitted, as true artists are obliged to do, that the male body displays harmonies of proportion and melodies of outline more comprehensive, more indicative of strength expressed in terms of grace, than that of women. 1 I guard myself against saying--more seductive to the senses, more soft, more delicate, more undulating. The superiority of male beauty does not consist in these attractions, but in the symmetrical development of all the qualities of the human frame, the complete organisation of the body as the supreme instrument of vital energy. In the bloom of adolescence the elements of feminine grace, suggested rather than expressed, are combined with virility to produce a perfection which is lacking to the mature and adult excellence of either sex. The Greek lover, if I am right in the idea which I have formed of him, sought less to stimulate desire by the contemplation of sensual charms than to attune his spirit with the spectacle of strength at rest in suavity. He admired the chastened lines, the figure slight but sinewy, the limbs well-knit and flexible, the small head set upon broad shoulders, the keen eyes, the austere reins, and the elastic movement of a youth made vigorous by exercise. Physical perfection of this kind suggested to his fancy all that he loved best in moral qualities. Hardihood, self-discipline, alertness of intelligence, health, temperance, indomitable spirit, energy, the joy of active life, plain living and high thinking--these qualities the Greeks idealised, and of these, "the lightning vision of the darling," was the living incarnation. There is plenty in their literature to show that paiderastia obtained sanction from the belief that a soul of this sort would be found within the body of a young man rather than a woman. I need scarcely add that none but a race of artists could be lovers of this sort, just as none but a race of poets were adequate to apprehend the chivalrous enthusiasm for woman as an object of worship.

The morality of the Greeks, as I have tried elsewhere to prove, was æsthetic. They regarded humanity as a part of a good and beautiful universe, nor did they shrink from any of their normal instincts. To find the law of human energy, the measure of man's natural desires, the right moment for indulgence and for self-restraint, the balance which results in health, the proper limit for each several function which secures the harmony of all, seemed to them the aim of ethics. Their personal code of conduct ended in "modest self-restraint:" not abstention, but selection. and subordination ruled their practice. They were satisfied with controlling much that more ascetic natures unconditionally suppress. Consequently, to the Greeks there was nothing at first sight criminal in paiderastia. To forbid it as a hateful and unclean thing did not occur to them. Finding it within their hearts, they chose to regulate it, rather than to root it out. It was only after the inconveniences and scandals to which paiderastia gave rise had been forced upon their notice, that they felt the visitings of conscience and wavered in their fearless attitude.

In like manner the religion of the Greeks was æsthetic. They analysed the world of objects and the soul of man, unconsciously perhaps, but effectively, and called their generalisations by the names of gods and goddesses. That these were beautiful and filled with human energy was enough to arouse in them the sentiments of worship. The notion of a single Deity who ruled the human race by punishment and favour, hating certain acts while he tolerated others--in other words, a God who idealised one part of man's nature to the exclusion of the rest--had never passed into the sphere of Greek conceptions. When, therefore, paiderastia became a fact of their consciousness, they reasoned thus: If man loves boys, God loves boys also. Homer and Hesiod forgot to tell us about Ganymede and Hyacinth and Hylas. Let these lads be added to the list of Danaë and Semele and Io. Homer told us that, because Ganymede was beautiful, Zeus made him the serving-boy of the immortals. We understand the meaning of that tale. Zeus loved him. The reason why he did not leave him here on earth like Danaë was that he could not beget sons upon his body and people the earth with heroes. Do not our wives stay at home and breed our children? "Our favourite youths" are always at our side.

Footnotes

68:1 The following passage may be extracted from a letter of Winckelmann (see Pater's *Studies in the History of the Renaissance*, p. 162): "As it is confessedly the beauty of man which is to be conceived under one general idea, so I have noticed that those who are observant of beauty only in women, and are moved little or not at all by the beauty of men, seldom have an impartial, vital, inborn instinct for beauty in art. To such persons the beauty of Greek art will ever seem wanting, because its supreme beauty is rather male than female." To this I think we ought to add that, while it is true that "the supreme beauty of Greek art is rather male than female," this is due not so much to any passion of the Greeks for male beauty as to the fact that the male body exhibits a higher organisation of the human form than the female.

XIX.

Sexual inversion among Greek women offers more difficulties than we met with in the study of paiderastia. This is due, not to the absence of the phenomenon, but to the fact that feminine homosexual passions were never worked into the social system, never became educational and military agents. The Greeks accepted the fact that certain females are congenitally indifferent to the male sex, and appetitive of their own sex. This appears from the myth of Aristophanes in Plato's *Symposium*, which expresses in comic form their theory of sexual differentiation. There were originally human beings of three sexes: men, the offspring of the sun; women, the offspring of the earth; hermaphrodites, the offspring of the moon. They were round with two faces, four hands, four feet, and two sets of reproductive organs apiece. In the case of the third (hermaphroditic or lunar) sex, one set of reproductive organs was male, the other female. Zeus, on account of the insolence and vigour of these primitive human creatures, sliced them into halves. Since that time the halves of each sort have always striven to unite with their corresponding halves, and have found some satisfaction in carnal congress--males with males, females with females, and (in the case of the lunar or hermaphroditic creatures) males and females with one another. Philosophically, then, the homosexual passion of female for female, and of male for male, was placed upon exactly the same footing as the heterosexual passion of each sex for its opposite. Greek logic admitted the homosexual female to equal rights with the homosexual male, and both to the same natural freedom as heterosexual individuals of either species.

Although this was the position assumed by philosophers, Lesbian passion, as the Greeks called it, never obtained the same social sanction as boy-love. It is significant that Greek mythology offers no legends of the goddesses parallel to those which consecrated paiderastia among the male deities. Again, we have no recorded example, so far as I can remember, of noble friendships between women rising into political and historical prominence. There are no female analogies to Harmodius and Aristogeiton, Cratinus and Aristodemus. It is true that Sappho and the Lesbian poetesses gave this female passion an eminent place in Greek literature. But the Æolian women did not found a glorious tradition corresponding to that of the Dorian men. If homosexual love between females assumed the form of an institution at one moment in Æolia, this failed to strike roots deep into the subsoil of the nation. Later Greeks, while tolerating, regarded it rather as an eccentricity of nature, or a vice, than as an honourable and socially useful emotion. The condition of women in ancient Hellas sufficiently accounts for the result. There was no opportunity in the harem or the zenana of raising homosexual passion to the same moral and spiritual efficiency as it obtained in the camp, the palæstra, and the schools of the philosophers. Consequently, while the Greeks utilised and ennobled boy-love, they left Lesbian love to follow the same course of degeneracy as it pursues in modern times.

In order to see how similar the type of Lesbian love in ancient Greece was to the form which it assumed in modern Europe, we have only to compare Lucian's Dialogues with Parisian tales by Catulle Mendès or Guy de Maupassant. The woman who seduces the girl she loves, is, in the girl's phrase, "over-masculine," "androgynous." The Megilla of Lucian insists upon being called Megillos. The girl is a weaker vessel, pliant, submissive to the virago's sexual energy, selected from the class of meretricious *ingénues*.

There is an important passage in the *Amores* of Lucian which proves that the Greeks felt an abhorrence of sexual inversion among women similar to that which moderns feel for its manifestation among men. Charicles, who supports the cause of normal heterosexual passion, argues after this wise:

"If you concede homosexual love to males, you must in justice grant the same to females; you will have to sanction carnal intercourse between them; monstrous instruments of lust will have to be permitted, in order that their sexual congress may be carried out; that obscene vocable, tribad, which so rarely offends our ears--I blush to utter it--will become rampant, and Philænis will spread androgynous orgies throughout our harems."

What these monstrous instruments of lust were may be gathered from the sixth mime of Herodas, where one of them is described in detail. Philænis may, perhaps, be the poetess of an obscene book on sensual refinements, to whom Athenæus alludes (*Deinosophistæ*, viii, 335). It is also possible that Philænis had become the common designation of a Lesbian lover, a tribad. In the later periods of Greek literature, as I have elsewhere shown, certain fixed masks of Attic comedy (corresponding to the masks of the Italian *Commedia dell' Arte*) created types of character under conventional names--so that, for example, Cerdo became a cobbler, Myrtalë a common whore, and possibly Philænis a Lesbian invert.

The upshot of this parenthetic, al investigation is to demonstrate that, while the love of Males for males in Greece obtained moralisation, and reached the high position of a recognised social function, the love of female for female remained undeveloped and unhonoured, on the same level as both forms of homosexual passion in the, modern European world are.

XX.

Greece merged in Rome; but, though the Romans aped the arts and manners of the Greeks., they never truly caught the Hellenic spirit. Even Virgil only trod the court of the Gentiles of Greek culture. It was not, therefore, possible that any social custom so peculiar as paiderastia should flourish on Latin soil. Instead of Cleomenes and Epameinondas, we find at Rome Nero the bride of Sporus and Commodus the public prostitute. Alcibiades is replaced by the Mark Antony of Cicero's *Philippic*. Corydon, with artificial notes, takes up the song of Ageanax. The melodies of Meleager are drowned in the harsh discords of Martial. Instead of love, lust was the deity of the boy-lover on the shores of Tiber.

In the first century of the Roman Empire Christianity began its work of reformation. When we estimate the effect of Christianity, we must bear in mind that the early Christians found Paganism disorganised and humanity rushing to a precipice of ruin. Their first efforts were directed toward checking the sensuality of Corinth, Athens, Rome, the capitals of Syria and Egypt. Christian asceticism, in the corruption of the Pagan systems, led logically to the cloister and the hermitage. The component elements of society had been disintegrated by the Greeks in their decadence, and by the Romans in their insolence of material prosperity. To the impassioned followers of Christ nothing was left but separation from nature, which had become incurable in its monstrosity of vices. But the convent was a virtual abandonment of social problems.

From this policy of despair, this helplessness to cope with evil and this hopelessness of good on earth, emerged a new and nobler synthesis, the merit of which belongs in no small measure to the Teutonic converts to the Christian faith. The Middle Ages proclaimed through chivalry the truth, then for the first time fully apprehended, that woman is the mediating and ennobling element in human life. Not in escape into the cloister, not in the self-abandonment to vice, but in the fellow-service of free men and women must be found the solution of social problems. The mythology of Mary gave religious sanction to the chivalrous enthusiasm; and a cult of woman sprang into being to which, although it was romantic and visionary, we owe the spiritual basis of our domestic and civil life. The *modus vivendi* of the modern world was found.

FINIS.

Printed in Great Britain
by Amazon